Starting to turn and meaning to yell for Escalier to stop, Beatriz felt a shove which sent her reeling clear of any possible danger. Before she could stop, or even turn her head to find out what was happening, it was over.

While Ole Devil's left hand was thrusting the woman aside, his right flew across and enfolded the concave handle of his bowie knife. Bending his knees and twisting around as he was drawing the weapon, he lowered his torso sufficiently to allow the sabre to pass over his head. Having taken that precaution, he turned his hand with the thumb downwards and lunged. Converging with the onrushing officer, who could do nothing to avoid his fate, the clip point passed between two of his left ribs and sank onwards until it found his heart.

Shoving himself to the right, Ole Devil snatched the blade free and allowed Escalier to go down. Nothing on the young Texan's face showed his grim satisfaction. One of the men responsible for the massacre at Goliad had paid the price.

Ole Devil doubted whether any of the others, particularly Urrea, would be so easy.

Also by J. T. EDSON

Ole Devil Hardin Stories:
YOUNG OLE DEVIL
OLE DEVIL AND
   THE CAPLOCKS †
GET URREA

Civil War Stories:
COMANCHE
YOU'RE IN COMMAND
   NOW MR. FOG
THE BIG GUN
UNDER THE STARS AND BARS
THE FASTEST GUN IN TEXAS
KILL DUSTY FOG!
THE DEVIL GUN
THE COLT AND THE SABRE
THE REBEL SPY
THE BLOODY BORDER
BACK TO THE BLOODY BORDER

The Floating Outfit Stories:
THE YSABEL KID
.44 CALIBRE MAN
A HORSE CALLED MOGOLLON
GOODNIGHT'S DREAM
FROM HIDE AND HORN
SET TEXAS BACK ON HER FEET
THE RIDE AND TALLOW MEN
THE HOODED RIDERS
QUIET TOWN
TRAIL BOSS
WAGONS TO BACKSIGHT
TROUBLED RANGE
SIDEWINDER
RANGELAND HERCULES
MCGRAW'S INHERITANCE
THE HALF-BREED
THE WILDCATS
THE BAD BUNCH
THE FAST GUN
CUCHILO
A TOWN CALLED YELLOWDOG
TRIGGER FAST
THE MAKING OF A LAWMAN
THE TROUBLE BUSTERS
THE LAW OF THE GUN
THE PEACEMAKERS
TO ARMS, TO ARMS, IN DIXIE!
HELL IN THE PALO DURO
GO BACK TO HELL
THE SOUTH WILL RISE AGAIN
SET A-FOOT †
THE RUSHERS
THE QUEST FOR
   BOWIE'S BLADE
THE FORTUNE HUNTERS
THE HARD RIDERS
THE RIO HONDO KID
WACO'S DEBT
THE TEXAN
THE FLOATING OUTFIT
APACHE RAMPAGE
RIO GUNS
RIO HONDO WAR
GUNSMOKE THUNDER

THE MAN FROM TEXAS
GUN WIZARD
THE SMALL TEXAN
THE TOWN TAMERS
RETURN TO BACKSIGHT
TERROR VALLEY
GUNS IN THE NIGHT

Waco Stories:
SAGEBRUSH SLEUTH
ARIZONA RANGER
WACO RIDES IN
THE DRIFTER
DOC LEROY M.D. †
HOUND-DOG MAN

Calamity Jane Stories:
GOLD DECK, HOT LEAD
CALAMITY SPELLS TROUBLE
TROUBLE TRAIL
THE BULL WHIP BREED
THE COW THIEVES
WHITE STALLION, RED MARE
THE WHIP AND
   THE WAR LANCE †
THE BIG HUNT

John Slaughter Stories:
SLAUGHTER'S WAY
SLAUGHTER'S NEIGHBOURS †

*Brady Anchor and Jefferson Trade
Stories:*
TWO MILES TO THE BORDER
WHO DO YOU TRUST,
   UNCLE BRADY? †

Waxahachie Smith Stories:
NO FINGER ON THE TRIGGER †
SLIP GUN
WAXAHACHIE SMITH †
CURE THE TEXAS FEVER †

Rockabye County Stories:
SIXTEEN DOLLAR SHOOTER
THE SHERIFF OF
   ROCKABYE COUNTY †
THE PROFESSIONAL KILLERS
THE ¼ SECOND DRAW
THE DEPUTIES
POINT OF CONTACT
THE OWLHOOT
RUN FOR THE BORDER
BAD HOMBRE
THEY CALL IT PROGRESS †

*The School Swot Stories Written in
collaboration with Peter Clawson:*
BLONDE GENIUS

Bunduki Stories:
BUNDUKI
BUNDUKI AND DAWN

published by CORGI BOOKS
† to be published by CORGI BOOKS

No. 77 Get Urrea

J. T. Edson

CORGI BOOKS
A DIVISION OF TRANSWORLD PUBLISHERS LTD

NO. 77 GET URREA
A CORGI BOOK 0 552 09905 8

First publication in Great Britain

PRINTING HISTORY
Corgi edition published 1975

Corgi Books are published by
Transworld Publishers Ltd.,
Cavendish House, 57–59 Uxbridge Road,
Ealing, London W.5.
Made and printed in the United States of America
by Arcata Graphics,
Buffalo, New York

For all the members of the White Lion
Shooting, Fishing and Beer Drinking Society

Author's note:

I would like to apologise to fictionist geneaologist Philip Jose Farmer for the printing error which names him 'Frazer' on Page 205 of THE QUEST FOR BOWIE'S BLADE.

CHAPTER ONE
None Of Them Must Get Away!

CARRYING what little remained of their personal belongings in bundles on their shoulders, some four hundred men were trudging along a trail that passed through the bottom of a woodland valley about four miles to the north-east of Goliad. Most of them were, if not happy, at least relieved by the change in their circumstances. For all that, a sense of failure prevented them from displaying joy or satisfaction. Each of them was engrossed in his own thoughts as they walked in four ragged files.

It was Palm Sunday, March the 27th, 1836. Six days earlier, the men in the column had partially destroyed Fort Defiance and had belatedly set off to try and join the main body of the newly-created Republic of Texas Army on the Colorado River. Already demoralized by the vacillation and inept leadership of their commanding officer Colonel James W. Fannin, they had put up only a token resistance when surrounded in open country by General José Urrea's Tamaulipa Brigade. Apparently their lack of aggression before surrendering had saved them from meeting the fate of the defenders of the Alamo Mission at San Antonio, who had been wiped out to a man after a siege lasting thirteen days which had cost other units of the Mexican Army many hundreds of lives.

Instead of receiving similar treatment, Fannin and his men had been returned to Fort Defiance and held there. Six miserable and worrying days had dragged by until, the previous evening, an offer had been made to them.

9

If they would give their parole not to resume fighting against the Mexican Government and to quit Texas for ever, they would be set free and escorted to safety. Suspecting that a refusal might have tragic results, Fannin and the majority of the officers had advised their men to accept. Although there were a few who had had doubts, they had concurred rather than jeopardize the chances of their companions.

Lieutenant Paul Dimmock was one who had misgivings. Having lived among Mexicans for five years before the Texians* had been driven to open rebellion by the oppressions of the tyrannical dictator, *Presidente* Antonio Lopez de Santa Anna,† he was puzzled by the apparent leniency being shown by their captors. It was not in keeping with the treatment usually accorded to *el Presidente's* enemies. He did not have a reputation for being merciful, or forgiving, to those who opposed his will.

For all Dimmock's doubts, he had to admit that Urrea appeared to be keeping the conditions of their release. While their weapons had not been returned to them, which was only to be expected, they had not been robbed of their personal property. In addition, to protect them from molestation by other members of the Mexican Army who did not know their status, a troop of the Tamaulipa Lancers were escorting them.

From his place in the left hand column, Dimmock found himself looking past the officer in front of him towards the rear section of the escort's advance guard. Instead of being comforted by the sight of the lance-armed riders, sitting with easy competence on their big horned, slick-forked, low cantled and single girthed sad-

---

* *Texian: the name given to an Anglo-U.S.-born settler in Texas, the 'i' being dropped from usage after the Mexican War of 1846/48.*

† *An explanation of why the Texians were driven to rebel is given in: YOUNG OLE DEVIL.*

dles, he felt a vague uneasiness which he
quell or satisfy. His instincts insisted that
wrong, but just what it might be he cou

There was, although the lieutenant did not know it, considerable justification for his suspicions and concern.

Riding his fine bay gelding at the front of the slowly moving column, as befitted the commanding officer of the escort, Major Carlos Badillo was studying the wood-covered slopes with considerable satisfaction. Everything was as planned. Nobody had forgotten the instructions which had been given to them. That was not entirely surprising as they all knew he was responsible for the orders. He had already built up a reputation for being a ruthless martinet which spread through the whole of the Tamaulipa Brigade and made him feared far more than many officers superior to him in rank.

Not quite six foot in height, Badillo had a slender build and a swift flowing grace of movement which could have brought him much acclaim as a bullfighter. Not yet thirty, and despite a certain antipathy which existed towards men of pure and high Spanish birth in the new Mexico that had gained its independence from Spain in 1822, his cold courage and ruthless nature had carried him to field rank in a regiment that had become noted for its bravery and ability in battle.

A high crowned, short peaked, black *shako* tilted at a rakish angle on Badillo's head. One inch wide white bands encircled the top and bottom of the crown and a silver Mexican eagle badge glinted at the front. A silver-scaled chinstrap framed exceptionally handsome features. The cold dark eyes and lips normally held a sardonic, humourless smile that were warning of the cruelty and savagery behind them. Cut from the finest cloth to show off his build to its best advantage, his waist-long dark green tunic had a deep red chest and facings. Its shoulder scales (denoting his rank) and other metal work were made from silver. Tight-legged

11

d bell-bottomed, after the fashion of a *vaquero*, his trousers were also of dark green and had a red stripe running down each outer seam. Large rowelled and elegantly made spurs graced the heels of his sharply pointed black boots. Unlike the enlisted men, who were armed with nine foot long lances, he carried a finely made sabre on the slings at the left side of his glossily-polished black leather waist belt.

Satisfied that all was as it should be, Badillo slackened the grip of his left fingers slightly on the one-piece reins. While the fingers of his right fist went across to curl around the hilt of his sabre, his heels gave a gentle tap which signalled his well trained mount to go a little faster. Behind him, dressed in a similar fashion—although the materials were of poorer quality—the half of his troop which formed the advance guard duplicated his actions. Knowing what to expect the enlisted men ensured that they were settled firmly in their saddles and then began to lift the butts of their lances from the metal socket that was attached to each man's right stirrup.

Following the instructions which he had received the previous afternoon while studying the trail with his superiors, Badillo's second-in-command signalled for the rear guard to slow down. Until then he had set a pace which compelled the Texians at the rear of the column to step lively so as to avoid being ridden down. With their companions at the front controlled by the advance guard's more leisurely gait, they had become bunched compactly instead of being allowed to straggle over a greater distance.

Absorbed by his attempts to work out what was puzzling him, Dimmock did not become aware of the column's compression until just after Badillo had begun to increase the bay's speed. By then, the burly enlisted man to the lieutenant's rear was almost treading on his heels and the blanket-wrapped bundle carried by the

12

captain in front of him was threatening to bump into his face.

Although Dimmock was not a professional soldier, he had sufficient military training to be aware how dangerous such bunching could be on the march. They were passing through terrain ideally suited for the laying of an ambush. There was enough cover on either side of the trail to conceal a regiment and the Mexicans were notorious for favouring such tactics.

Even as the lieutenant was contemplating the situation, he remembered that he was a prisoner on parole being escorted to safety and not a soldier marching through potentially hostile country. At the same moment, he noticed that the advance guard were drawing away. However, from his position in the column, he could not see that they were lifting their lances from the stirrup boots. Failing to see this he felt no more than a horseman's resentment over watching others riding when he had to walk and carry his belongings instead of letting his mount do it.

With his thoughts running in this direction, Dimmock realized what it was that struck him as unusual.

The Lancers had no bedrolls attached to the cantles of their saddles!

Even with that deficiency noticed, the full significance of it did not strike Dimmock immediately. Then, slowly, he began to realize what the omission suggested.

Badillo's troop had been assigned to accompany the parolees until they were beyond the rest of the Mexican Army's advance. Which meant that, travelling at the pace of men on foot, they would expect to be away from their regiment for at least a week and probably longer. Yet they were not carrying blankets, nor any of the other things which they would need for such an extensive absence.

Nothing Dimmock had seen or heard of the Tamaulipa Lancers led him to assume that they knew no better than to make such an error. They were, in fact, well known as a regiment with long experience in the field. It had been gained during the various rebellions, uprisings and struggles for power that had plagued Mexico since independence had been wrested from Spain. Such hardened veterans would not set off on a journey without carrying adequate means to ensure themselves of protection against the elements.

Unless, of course, they did not expect to be away from their base camp for more than a few hours and intended to be back by nightfall.

That could only apply under the present conditions if——

Dimmock's understanding of the situation came just too late!

Even as the lieutenant was about to start expressing his doubts and fears, movements and noises on the left side slope attracted his attention. Turning his gaze that way, he found the answer to why the Lancers had not troubled to bring their bedrolls. They must have known there was no need for them to do so. Clearly the column was not intended to go any further and the parole the Texians had been offered was no more than a means to lull them into a sense of false security.

Armed men were appearing from behind the bushes, trees and rocks where they had been crouching in concealment under the threat of severe punishment to any who allowed themselves to be seen and gave the ambush prematurely away.

Despite the urgency of the moment and the shock of his discovery, which none of his companions appeared to share, Dimmock's mind was instinctively recording certain facts regarding the men on the slope. Although they were wearing the cheap white canvas trousers of the Mexican *peons*, they were not the recently conscripted, inexperienced and poorly trained *Activos* reservists frequently thrown into action to take the brunt of the enemies' fire. They had taken off their bulky old pattern shakoes with the brass plate badge, scales, and red, white and blue plume of their national colours, but the red collar, piping, epaulettes, turnbacks and cuffs of their 'Turkish blue' coats told that they were regular infantry.

The weapons held by the enlisted men were further evidence of their status. Attached to the muzzles and ready for use, the long 'sword-bayonets' proved that they were armed with British Baker rifles and not the old, smoothbore Tower 'Brown Bess' muskets purchased from England to be issued to the *Activos*.

There was further evidence that the infantrymen's presence had not come about by accident. After having selected their places of concealment with the skill of experienced campaigners, in addition to discarding their headdresses, they had laid aside their wooden canteens and the cowhide packs in which they carried their personal belongings, and the rolled blanket strapped across the top. Each man, as he lined his rifle, was encumbered only by the empty bayonet scabbard and tin cartridge box suspended from his white crossbelts. They could move quickly and with ease after they had discharged their single shot weapons.

Standing at the side of a clump of bushes half way up the right hand slope from where he had been able to keep the whole of the ambush area under observation, Colonel Sebastian Saucedo studied the distances separating the two portions of the mounted escort of the Texians' column. Deciding that they were far enough away for *his* purposes, he prepared to give the order to open fire. If there should be any mishap, he would be able to counter the complaints by pointing out that every member of the 'Landero' Line Infantry Battalion had carried out his duties correctly.

Although Saucedo had two hundred and fifty enlisted men and their officers disposed in the area, such had

been their strict attention to orders and careful place-
ment under his supervision that not one of them had
shown himself until receiving the signal to do so. The
colonel was confident that, no matter what else might
happen, they would continue to perform the tasks
assigned to them in the same satisfactory manner. That
was, he told himself with relish as he began to raise the
sword in his right hand, the difference between soldiers
who were led by a fighting officer and fancily dressed
'gentlemen' following an arrogant and self-opinionated
dandy.

There was little love lost between the two officers who
were responsible for carrying out the somewhat ambigu-
ous instructions General Urrea had received from Santa
Anna regarding the disposal of their prisoners. Where
Badillo looked like what he was, a member of the
wealthy land-owning upper class, Saucedo's origins
stemmed from a much lower section of society. Everything about him showed that he was clearly 'of the
people'.

Of medium height, stocky and, despite running to fat
a trifle, powerfully built, the colonel's leathery, heavily
moustached and badly shaven face was coarse, hard
and cruel. Unlike Badillo, he made no attempt to dress
smartly. Apart from his insignia of rank being of tar-
nished silver, his uniform—which he appeared to have
both slept and ate in—was of no better quality than
those of the men under his command. The heavy calibre
flintlock pistol in his left fist was a plain, serviceable
weapon and there was nothing dainty about his sword.
It was designed for hacking rather than fancy work with
the point or wielding from a saddle. In fact, his clothing
and boots were better adapted to walking than riding.
Unlike the majority of his contemporaries in the Infantry, he invariably marched on foot with his men instead
of accompanying them mounted on a horse.

It was Saucedo's frequent boast that he had risen

through the ranks and he rarely troubled to conceal his antipathy towards officers who had not. Such an attitude did not endear him to the subjects of his scorn, but he never allowed their animosity to worry him. Commanding the best armed and toughest infantry battalion in the Tamaulipa Brigade, he had little to fear as long as he remained high in Urrea's favour.

Only one factor spoiled the colonel's satisfaction at having been given his present assignment. Despite his objections, he was compelled to work in close conjunction with Badillo. That Urrea had insisted upon the major taking part was worrying. It implied that the general held the major, who was everything Saucedo hated and despised, in considerable esteem and was willing to accede to his suggestions. However, the colonel believed that he could bring about the removal of his rival if certain arrangements he had made were successful. At the worst, Badillo might be blamed should anything go wrong with the ambush.

Shocked both by what he saw and the realization of its implications, Dimmock froze in mid-stride. Before he could return his raised right foot to the ground or yell a warning to his companions, the burly enlisted man following closely on his heels walked into him. The collision sent the lieutenant staggering, causing him to lose his balance and be knocked out of the column. Unable to recover his equilibrium, he sprawled face forward towards the side of the trail.

In doing so, his life was saved.

'Fire!' Saucedo commanded in a stentorian bellow, waving his sword as a signal in case the word did not carry to those of his men who were on the opposite side of the valley.

Two hundred and twenty-five fingers tightened on triggers. Set free, the same number of hammers swung around, the flints in their jaws striking sparks from the frizzens of the Baker rifles and igniting the powder in the priming pans. Set off by the sparks of flame which passed through the vents, the cartridges' charges turned into vast masses of gas. With a rippling roar, caused by the slight variations of time between the individual ignitions, the weapons on both sides of the valley vomited their loads at the mass of Texians.

Instantly, pandemonium reigned!

Fired from distances of between fifty and a hundred yards, not one of the shots missed finding its billet in human flesh. Taken unawares, many men went down dead or dying as the .70 calibre soft lead bullets ploughed into them. As might have been expected, although a few in the centre were struck down, most of the casualties occurred in the outer files. Hit in the head, Fannin fell without learning of the terrible fate into which he had led his men.

After watching the swathe of Texians going down before his battalion's deadly cross-fire, Saucedo flickered glances at the two parties of Lancers. Much to his annoyance, he discovered that his hopes in regard to them had not materialized. While their horses were startled by the commotion, they had been sufficiently prepared to avert the trouble he had desired. Although a few of them were having difficulties, the majority were in control of their mounts. In fact, some of the advance guard—especially Badillo, the colonel saw to his annoyance—were already starting to turn back. The men at the rear were lowering their lances so as to ride forward and help complete the slaughter.

'Charge!' Saucedo thundered and sprang forward, waving the sword above his head. 'At the bastards! None of them must get away!'

Flourishing pistols and swords, yelling encouragement, the rest of the officers led the rush towards the trail. Behind them, needing no urging, the enlisted men who had fired leapt into motion to the accompaniment of awe-inspiring whoops and bellows. However, twelve men on the right side and thirteen along the left remained in their positions. The best shots in the battalion, their weapons were still loaded and it was their duty to shoot down any Texian who managed to break clear of the attackers.

Even as Dimmock was going down, he heard the roaring of the Baker rifles. It was followed by the eerie sound of a bullet passing so close above him that he felt the wind of its passing. Then came the soggy impact of lead striking human flesh, screams of agony and yells of alarm. However, the lieutenant was one of the very few in the left hand file to come through the holocaust unscathed.

Striking the ground, still hardly able to believe that such a thing could be happening, Dimmock's first instinct was to rise. But at that point he heard, faintly yet with a terrible clarity due to the volume of power with which it had been made, Saucedo's bellowed order over the sounds of the stricken column. Taking a quick glance, the lieutenant saw the Mexican infantrymen pouring down the slope. They held their rifles with bayonets to the fore and were clearly determined to continue the slaughter that their bullets had begun.

Much as Dimmock wanted to spring to his feet and throw himself at the attackers, he realized that to do so would be useless. He would die before he could achieve anything. It was far more sensible to lie still, playing 'possum* until a chance of escape presented itself. If he could break clear, he would carry news of the massacre to the rest of the Republic of Texas's Army on the Colorado River. General Houston would not be able to do anything about avenging Fannin's command, but he would at least know that he could no longer count on their support.

---

* *Playing 'possum: the opossum*, Didelphis Marsupialis, *was famous for its habit of pretending to be dead when frightened or captured.*

Having reached his decision, Dimmock exerted all his will power so that he might carry it out. Clenching his fists and gritting his teeth, he forced himself to lie still as he heard the footsteps of the Mexican infantrymen rushing nearer.

Behind the lieutenant, the other Texians had been numbed into a state of immobility by the horror of what was happening. Then a full understanding of their deadly peril began to strike the survivors of the fusillade. Even those who had favoured the original surrender realized that they would not ever be allowed to fight again. With that knowledge, they prepared to sell their lives as dearly as possible.

Despite some difficulty in controlling his horse, Badillo's second-in-command was leading the rear guard forward. Slightly taller and heavier built than his superior, Captain Alphonso Escalier was greasily handsome, a dandy limited by his lack of money. His face was contorted with blood lust as he sent his mount forward and slashed with his sabre at the nearest Texian's head. Behind him, his men were fanning out so as to be able to use their lances.

Advancing with reckless bounds, an infantryman drew ahead of his companions. He had been one of the closest to the trail, so reached it first. Wild with excitement and a desire to kill, he decided that he would plunge his bayonet into the back of the Texian who was sprawled face down in front of him. Coming into range, he swung up his weapon and prepared to drive it at Dimmock.

CHAPTER TWO
Don't Let Him Escape!

BEFORE the infantryman could carry out his intention, a Texian from the second file intervened. Seeing that the soldier was about to bayonet the apparently helpless officer, who had been very popular and well-liked, the man sprang forward. As he did so, he swung the bundle from his shoulder and hurled it at the Mexican. Instead of driving his bayonet downwards, the soldier used it to deflect the approaching missile. Impaling the bundle, he flung it over his head. Before he returned the weapon to a fighting position, the Texian was upon him. Grabbing hold of the Baker rifle and wrenching it from its owner's grasp, the Texian smashed the butt against his head. As the infantryman went down with a crushed skull, his killer fell to a pistol in the hand of the nearest Mexican officer. With the rifle slipping from his lifeless hands, the Texian toppled alongside the man whose life he had saved.

Although Lieutenant Paul Dimmock had seen enough to guess what was happening, he forced himself to keep still. It went bitterly against the grain for a man of his background and upbringing to have to act in such a manner, particularly as the sounds of the fighting increased, but he continued to follow the course he had set himself. There was, he knew, more than the lives of his companions in the balance and his efforts would do little or nothing to prevent them from being killed. On the other hand, unless General Samuel Houston learned of the massacre, the rest of the Republic of Texas's Army would be in deadly peril. So Dimmock repeatedly reminded himself of that fact and compelled himself to remain motionless.

A savage hand to hand battle was soon raging on the trail. Despite the devastating effect of the murderous fusilade, sufficient of the Texians had escaped death or injury for them to equal the numbers of Colonel Sebastian Saucedo's 'Landero' Line Infantry Battalion. Of course, although hampered by the nature of their weapons, the troop of Tamaulipa Lancers gave the attackers a numerical superiority which made victory over the unarmed Texians practically certain. Even so, the Mexicans did not have things all their own way.

Weaponless, shocked and horrified by their captors' treachery and the cold-blooded murder of so many of their companions, the Texians started to fight back with a courage born of desperation and fury. Some of them tackled the charging foot soldiers, trying to avoid the enlisted men's bayonets or officers' swords and grapple with the wielders. Others flung themselves at the Lancers who were thrusting with their weapons at any figure which did not wear a Mexican uniform.

Soon the noise reached the proportions of bedlam. Men of both nationalities shouted, cursed, roared and screamed. Driven into the swirling mass of fighting human beings, horses snorted and squealed in terror as they smelled blood. Some bolted, their riders dragged from the saddles to add to the confusion. Two of the animals went down, plunging and kicking in agony, as wildly thrust bayonets impaled them instead of the proposed human targets. There were a few shots, fired from the pistols which Saucedo's officers and Captain Escalier were using to augment the slashing and hacking of their swords.

Having succeeded in bringing his bay gelding around in a half circle, Major Carlos Badillo found that he was obstructed by the other members of the advance guard who were also attempting to return and take a part in the fighting. There was no chance of him forcing his way through their ranks. Nor, obedient as they were under normal circumstances, would calling for them to let him pass be likely to produce the desired result. They were too excited for words to have any effect. So, instead of trying to do either, he completed the drawing of his sabre and guided his mount to the right with the intention of going around them.

The major's eagerness was caused by more than his sadistic delight in inflicting pain and killing. While he was starting to turn back, he had seen Saucedo bounding down the opposite slope. The colonel had already plunged into the thickest part of the fighting, just as the major had anticipated he would.

When helping to make the plans for the ambush, Badillo had known that the tactics he proposed would result in just such a fight as had developed. He was hoping to use the confusion of close quarters brawling as a means of removing his hated rival.

Given an opportunity, Badillo intended to kill Saucedo. He had decided that it must be done with one of the pistols which hung in their holsters on the pommel of his saddle. In that way, even if anybody should happen to see him do it, he could claim that the shot had been fired at a Texian and hit the colonel by accident. No doubt the truth would be suspected, but General Urrea would be unlikely to make too close an inquiry into what had really happened. With Saucedo dead, there was nobody else who had sufficient authority, or influence, to carry the matter further. Not even Badillo's own colonel. The major had gained such a moral ascendancy over his nominal superior that *he* was the commanding officer of the Tamaulipa Lancers in everything but name.

Although the major did not know it, he was in considerable danger as he started to ride by his men. He was not the only one to have foreseen the possibilities of removing a rival in the present situation.

Tall, lanky, with sharp and evil features, Sergeant Refugio was the best shot in the 'Landero' Line Infantry Battalion. His skill with the Baker rifle was one reason why he had been given command of the party who had remained on the left side slope to deal with any Texians who tried to escape. For all that, when three of them burst from the entangled mass and fled in his direction, he left the shooting to his men. Such behaviour would

23

have surprised anybody who knew him, for he usually enjoyed displaying his skill with a rifle.

There was a very good reason for Refugio to refrain from shooting. To reload the Baker could not be done quickly and he had a better use for the solitary bullet than expending it on a Texian. When assigning the duty to the sergeant, Saucedo had supplemented it with private instructions and the promise of promotion if he should be successful in carrying them out. There was, Refugio had considered, nothing difficult about his task. All he had to do was to watch for a suitable opportunity and then 'accidentally' shoot Major Badillo.

Holding the butt of the Baker rifle cradled at his shoulder and resting its thirty inch long barrel across a convenient limb as an aid to greater accuracy, the lanky sergeant scanned the ranks of the Lancers who had preceded the column. Luck appeared to be favouring him. Instead of riding through, or beyond, the rest of the advance guard, Badillo was coming along the left side of the valley. That meant he would pass at a distance of no more than seventy-five yards. An easy enough shot for a marksman like Sergeant—soon to be Captain—Refugio. All he had to do to earn his promotion was line his sights and, at the appropriate moment, squeeze the trigger.

To Refugio's way of thinking, selecting the correct moment was of considerable importance to his future. While he was not particularly intelligent, he had a certain amount of low cunning. Sufficient at least for him to be aware that his situation could be dangerous. Colonel Saucedo had promised that he would be protected against any repercussions, but he preferred not to take chances. Before he fired at Badillo, he wanted an excuse for shooting and, if possible, to have some of his men discharging their weapons at the same time. In that way, nobody would be able to say for sure whose bullet had struck the major down.

24

Keeping his decision in mind, Refugio sought for a way to carry out his assignment. Even as Badillo was approaching the point where he would be level with the sergeant's position, what appeared to be an ideal opportunity began to present itself.

On the fringe of the fighting, at the left side of the trail, a Texian was trying to save his younger brother's life. Avoiding the point of a lance as it was being driven in his direction, he caught hold of the shaft and tugged with all his strength. Unable to slip his wrist from the rawhide loop which was attached to the weapon's point of balance to enable a more secure grip when driving home the diamond-section head, the Lancer was hauled from his mount's back. As he fell he just managed to snatch his left foot out of the stirrup iron. However, he retained his hold on the reins and the jerk he gave at them snapped the animal's neck around, causing its legs to buckle and making it squeal with pain.

'Grab this hoss and go, Sam!' the elder brother bellowed, driving a kick against the side of the Lancer's head as he crashed to the ground and released the reins.

Remembering that their parents were getting on in years, had lost their home by accompanying Houston from San Antonio de Bexar and needed help to re-establish themselves elsewhere, still the younger brother hesitated for a moment. He hated the thought of fleeing as it meant leaving his sibling with little or no hope of escape. They had enlisted and served together and since the ambush began had been fighting back to back. Yet he knew that Tad was making a sensible suggestion and there was certainly no time to argue about which of them should leave.

Hurling a rifle, which he had wrenched from its owner's hands and used to defend himself, at the nearest Mexican foot soldier, Sam threw a sorrow-filled glance at his brother. Then he sprang to catch hold of the horse's saddlehorn and went astride its back with a bound. Grabbing up the one-piece reins, he let out a yell and kicked his heels against the animal's flanks. Already nervous due to the commotion and the hurt sustained when its former rider was unseated, the horse needed little urging. Trying to locate the stirrups with his feet and having difficulty keeping his balance, the young Texian found himself being carried towards what had been the head of the column.

Once again, good fortune was smiling upon Lieutenant Paul Dimmock, offering him the means by which he might carry out his self-appointed mission.

'Kill that one on the horse!' Refugio yelled, lining his rifle at Badillo and hoping for the desired result.

Even as he was shouting, the sergeant realized that he could not continue to rest the barrel on the branch. He had done so in the first place to lessen the strain of supporting the nine pound-two ounce* weapon while waiting and in case there should be a chance of aiming at a stationary target. With the major riding by, the added stability would be more of a liability than an asset. The Baker rifle was accurate up to about three hundred yards in skilled hands, but it had faults common to all flintlocks. One of these was the perceptible delay between squeezing the trigger and the detonated powder in the priming pan reaching the main charge.

Knowing his weapon's failings, Refugio did not keep the barrel pointing directly at his intended victim. Instead, having set it on to the required alignment, he aimed it ahead so as to allow for Badillo's forward movements. Waiting until he heard the crackle of shots from further along the slope, he squeezed the trigger. He continued to swing the rifle, holding it rock steady, so

---

Attaching the twenty-seven and a half inch long sword-bayonet, twenty-three inches of which was a single edged, spear-pointed blade, added an extra two pounds to the Baker Model of 1801's overall weight. It was not fixed when the rifle was required for accurate shooting at long range.

26

that the bullet would converge with the major on being ejected from the muzzle and traversing the distance between them.

Holding his bay to a swift half gallop that was carrying him by his men, Badillo did not suspect that his life was being threatened. He was scanning the tangled mass of fighting men, searching for Colonel Saucedó who had disappeared among them. He paid no attention to the slope above him.

Glancing ahead, the major noticed the young Texian emerging on the captured horse and decided to deal with him if the riflemen among the trees failed to do so. He heard Refugio's shouted command. It was followed by at least four shots. Thinking sourly of the wasted effort and possible danger to their own men who were fighting on the trail (although the latter did not greatly disturb him) Badillo saw that at least one of the bullets had flown accurately. Hit in the right temple, with the lead smashing straight through his head, the Texian was knocked sideways out of the saddle. However, the horse continued to run.

Although he was still lying on the ground, Dimmock was alert for any opportunity to escape. Without being detected, he had contrived to look around and ease himself into a position which would allow him to rise swiftly when he found his chance. He was aware of the purpose of the riflemen on the slope but did not know how many there might be. Seeing the young Texian killed and the horse approaching, he decided that he wouldn't have a better opportunity. So, waiting until it drew near, he thrust himself to his feet and leapt forward with his hands reaching to grab the reins.

Turning at the waist and guiding his weapon with the smooth ease of an expert, Refugio felt the solid thrust of the recoil against his right shoulder. Although the cloud of white smoke which gushed from the barrel obscured his view, he was confident that he had held true.

Only one small detail saved Badillo from a not undeserved death. The time that elapsed between the fall of the Baker's hammer and the emission of the bullet from the muzzle.

While the sergeant had believed there was a clear field of fire between himself and his victim, he had failed to notice a sapling further down the slope. Flying through the air at the correct angle to connect with its intended target, the bullet grazed the right side of the slender trunk. Slight though the contact had been, it was sufficient to deflect the patched lead ball.* Not much, but enough. Instead of striking Badillo in the body (Refugio having been disinclined to chance a shot at the smaller—if more certainly lethal—target of the head) it caught the bay just in front of the shoulder. Distorting from its globular shape as it ploughed through the flesh, the bullet hit and broke the bones of the horse's neck. Killed almost instantly, the animal crumpled and went down, falling on to its left side.

Hearing the sickening, soggy thud of the bullet's impact and feeling his mount collapsing beneath him, Badillo realized that it must have been shot. There was no time for him to wonder if the shooting had been accidental or a deliberate attempt to murder him. In fact, it was all he could do to liberate his feet from the stirrups and hurl himself out of the saddle so as to prevent having his left leg trapped. Because of the direction in which the animal was falling, he was unable to dive to the right. Instead, he was compelled to go down in front of the foremost of his men. While his skill as a rider enabled him to reduce some of the force of his landing,

---

* *Patched lead ball: a bullet which is wrapped in a small 'patch' made from cloth or very thin hide to ensure a tight fit in the rifling grooves of the barrel. The .70 calibre Baker fired a patched ball weighing twenty to the pound.*

and even though he had tossed aside his sabre as he fell, he still hit the ground hard enough to jar all the breath from his body. It left him sprawled dazed, winded and helpless not far ahead of the approaching Lancers' horses.

Although the horse that Dimmock was trying to catch attempted to shy away, his fingers made contact with its reins. He grasped the leather strap tenaciously with his left hand. At the same time, his right fist closed just as tightly over the saddlehorn. He felt a sudden jerk, but his grip held and he utilized the animal's forward momentum as a propulsive aid to making a swinging, leaping mount.

Even as the lieutenant felt the hard leather of the saddle between his legs, he knew that he was by no means out of danger. To escape, he must run the gauntlet of the riflemen on the slope and the much closer Lancers. Locating the stirrup irons and inserting his feet, he flattened himself alongside the horse's neck and guided it at an angle of about forty-five degrees. That would take him clear of the riders, but in ascending the slope, he might be approaching one of the infantrymen. It was, he realized, a chance he had to take.

At that moment, Refugio shot Badillo's horse and, in doing so, slightly reduced the danger to Dimmock.

Furious at having failed to kill the major, the lanky sergeant acted swiftly. He started to lower the rifle's butt with the intention of reloading as swiftly as possible. Once he had done so, he hoped he would be able to make another attempt at earning the promised promotion. Before he had time to make a start, he noticed Dimmock riding away from the trail.

'There's one of them getting away on a horse!' Refugio bawled, realizing that the lieutenant would pass him and that there was nobody further along the slope to stop him. 'Shoot the bastard!'

Much to the sergeant's annoyance, the order was not

obeyed. Snarling a curse, he turned his head to discover why he was being ignored. More by accident than deliberate choice, he had selected a position from which he could see the majority of his party. Every member of it within his range of vision was in a similar situation to himself. The butts of their rifles were on the ground and they were in various stages of recharging the barrels with powder and ball. Realizing the futility of trying to make them hurry up the process which was always laborious, Refugio gave a resigned shrug. He could see what was happening on the trail and decided that he would be able to transfer the blame on the Lancers if the Texian should escape.

Having their commanding officer flung headlong to the ground in front of them caused considerable inconvenience and some concern to the leading riders of what had been the advance guard. Despite his faults, Badillo had many qualities which appealed to the tough, hard-bitten erstwhile *vaqueros* and former *bandidos*—who had elected to join the Army rather than be imprisoned for their various crimes—serving under him. His undoubted courage, skill with weapons and deadly efficient way of enforcing his will upon others had won their admiration and respect. In addition, the more intelligent of them saw him as a leader who was rising in prominence and realized that it might be beneficial to support him.

So, wanting to save the major from further injury, the men acted with a greater speed than they would have displayed with a less favoured officer. Manipulating their reins, they contrived to either turn aside or halt their horses before reaching Badillo. In doing so, they threw the riders who were following them into some confusion. Those behind, including a few who had observed Dimmock riding off, were also compelled to hurriedly stop.

'Hey, you Lancers!' Refugio shouted at the top of his voice, his intention being to place the responsibility for the Texian's escape elsewhere. 'Our rifles are empty. Get after that one. Don't let him escape.'

Despite the warning, several seconds elapsed before a sergeant managed to force his horse from the tangle that had been caused by half the troop coming to a sudden stop. Five other men succeeded in extracting themselves and followed him.

Brief though the delay in starting the pursuit had been, it allowed Dimmock to build a slight but significant lead. What was more, he had heard and understood Refugio's words. They had been a source of relief to him. Unless the speaker was trying to lull him into a sense of false security, there was no danger of him being shot by the men on the slope.

Taking a chance that what he had heard was true, Dimmock raised his torso until he was sitting more erect on the saddle. This way he could control the horse with greater facility and also have a better view of his surroundings. The latter was of the greatest importance with respect to the line of action he was contemplating. No shots were fired at him and he concluded that the gamble had paid off.

Despite his conviction, the lieutenant kept a careful watch on the terrain ahead. Not only was he alert for obstructions to his flight, but he was also searching for any sign of Mexican infantrymen. Even one with an empty rifle could be a source of danger. However, he saw none and decided that he must have passed beyond the end of the screen of sharpshooters. Which meant he had only the pursuing Lancers to contend with.

There were, however, Dimmock reminded himself grimly, many long miles to be covered before he could hope to reach anything even approaching safety.

CHAPTER THREE
Now We've Got Him

HAVING avoided the fighting on the trail, and by-passed the 'Landero' Line Infantry Battalion's sharpshooters, Lieutenant Paul Dimmock gave all his attention to considering how he might evade his pursuers. He could hear some of the Tamaulipa Lancers coming after him, but he did not know how many he had to contend with. Nor did he attempt to look behind and satisfy his curiosity. Judging from the noise they were making, there were several of them. Too many, certainly, for him to be able to fight them off in his unarmed condition. So he concentrated his thoughts and energies on some other means of getting away.

While guiding his horse up the slope, Dimmock swiftly assessed the situation and drew his conclusions.

While not exactly hopeless, they were far from comforting!

Already the lieutenant's instincts as a rider had informed him that he was sitting a horse well endowed with what the Mexican *vaqueros* called *brio escondido*.* Unfortunately, the quality of the saddle and bridle suggested that it had belonged to an enlisted man rather than an officer. The supposition was supported by there being neither pistol nor rifle on the saddle. If the small amount of shooting that had taken place was any guide, only the officers had firearms. While the nine foot lances were effective weapons, Dimmock had gained sufficient lead to be out of reach of their sharp pointed steel heads. There was even, he realized, a way in which he might turn their armament to his advantage.

Instead of directing his horse towards the more open

---

* *Brio escondido: stamina and endurance of a high order.*

country, Dimmock sent it into the thicker woodland. Passing through it would be more difficult, with the danger of him being swept from the saddle by a branch. But against that, the Mexicans, encumbered by their lances, would find it even less easy to traverse such terrain.

Silently blessing the training and experience he had gained whilst following a pack of fast running foxhounds through the woodlands of Tennessee, Dimmock used every bit of the skill he had acquired as he urged his mount onwards. Ducking his head and swaying his torso, he dodged such boughs as might otherwise have dislodged him. Beneath his legs, the borrowed horse proved to be adept at travelling swiftly under such trying conditions. Ignoring the sudden alterations in its rider's weight and balance, it remained responsive to the signals it received through the bit in its mouth or the heels against its ribs. Nor did it run blindly, but was ready to avoid colliding with a tree whether instructed to do so or not.

Although they were just as well mounted, equally reckless, and skilled at riding, the six Mexicans found themselves falling behind their quarry. As the lieutenant had anticipated, they discovered that the lances were a great nuisance in woodland. However, discarding their weapons was out of the question. Only the sergeant carried a pistol. The rest had nothing more than their fighting knives as sidearms.

Dimmock's summation of the situation proved to be correct. On emerging from the woodland, he had increased his lead to around a quarter of a mile. Glancing back, as he allowed his mount to gallop across terrain which did not require constant surveillance, he counted the Lancers as they came into view. There were six of them, including a sergeant who was in the lead urging the rest to greater efforts. If Dimmock had been able to see at that distance he would have noticed that three had lost their shakoes and there was a bloody graze on the cheek of a fourth which suggested he had not been entirely successful in avoiding some kind of obstruction, but all of them still carried their lances. Even the injured man was showing no inclination of giving up the chase. Letting out excited whoops, they forced their horses to go faster as soon as they saw the Texian.

Making no attempt to return to the trail, Dimmock headed north across country. He could hear nothing of the desperate struggle which was still raging behind the woodland. Although he hated the idea of having deserted his hard-pressed companions, he knew it could not be helped. So resolutely he thrust the thought from his mind. There were other, equally important, matters demanding his undivided attention.

Firstly, Dimmock knew that he must throw the pursuing Lancers off his tracks. Then he would go on until he found the Colorado River, or some other landmark that would help him to locate the camp of the Republic of Texas's Army. If he was fortunate, he would meet up with one of its patrols or ranging—as scouting was called at that period—parties. However he was unlikely to receive help for several miles. In fact, it was unlikely that he would establish contact with any friendly force before at least the following afternoon. Perhaps not even then. It was rumoured that General Houston was disgusted with the continued failure of Colonel James W. Fannin's command and his inability to take any positive military action, and had therefore abandoned Fannin's men to their fate.

Even if the lieutenant should escape from the six Lancers, his position would be anything but a sinecure. He would also have to avoid any other Mexican units who might be operating between himself and his destination. In addition, there were other foes to be contended with. White renegades who served Santa Anna, indistinguishable in dress and appearance from loyal Texians but who were even more dangerous than regular soldiers or *Activos*. Traitors to their own kind, ruthless and cold-blooded, working for pay rather than out of more noble motives, they would not hesitate to capture or kill him. So he was determined to stay away from all human beings unless he could be absolutely sure of their sympathies.

After Dimmock had looked back to discover the number of his pursuers and how far they were behind, he returned his gaze to what lay ahead. Not only did he need to keep an eye on where he was going, he also had to watch out for anybody who might be ahead of him.

Keen huntsman as the lieutenant was, he had never before ridden as he did that day. Of course, the hunts had been merely for sport and enjoyment. For the first time, he found himself the quarry. Not that he gave his change of status much thought. He was far too busy utilizing every scrap of his experience as a horseman to strike the happy medium between staying well beyond the reach of the Mexicans' weapons and conserving sufficient of his mount's energy to produce extra speed should it be needed.

With the Lancers following (although they were unable to close the gap) Dimmock led the way northwards. Responding to his every signal, the horse he was riding proved that it did indeed have *brio escondido*. It ran swiftly for almost two miles, plunging catfooted down slopes, climbing others, weaving through bushes, hurdling streams or small obstacles in its path. Yet, for all the reckless pace it set, the Mexicans showed no sign of turning back.

Suddenly Dimmock became aware that the lathered horse was showing signs of distress. He did not know that its right hindquarters had been hurt when its original rider was dragged from the saddle. Although the injury had been slight, the continuous strain and effort was

35

beginning to aggravate it. It said much for the animal's spirit that the lieutenant had been carried so far and at such speed over the rolling plains.

With each successive sequence of hoof-beats in the galloping gait, Dimmock could feel the horse faltering. He knew that, gallant as it was, the pain would soon bring it to a stop. Nor could it be happening in a worse place. They were on open ground, with no cover closer than a large grove of post oaks about half a mile ahead along the top of a slope.

Studying the trees, Dimmock decided that if he could reach them he might still be able to escape. Once amongst them, he could find sufficient cover in which he could hide. There was a chance that, if the Mexicans split up to search for him, he might be able to jump one of them and obtain another mount. Failing that, provided he could avoid being located, he would continue his journey on foot once they had given up the search.

Unfortunately for the lieutenant, the horse could not carry him far enough to put his plans into effect. Despite all his efforts to keep it going, its pace grew slower. Seeing what was happening, the Lancers yelled their delight and urged their white-lathered mounts to greater speed.

At the foot of the fairly gentle slope, with the post oaks still over a hundred yards away and the Lancers about twice that distance behind, Dimmock's horse was done. It staggered, regained its balance, stumbled on for a few steps and came to a halt.

Knowing that the horse was finished, Dimmock removed his right foot from the stirrup and swung it forward over the saddle. He vaulted to the ground, landing running and headed up the incline.

'Now we've got him!' the sergeant whooped.

Although the words did not reach Dimmock, he knew that his predicament would put fresh heart into his pursuers. Guessing that they would be pushing their tired mounts even harder in their eagerness to end the long chase, he made towards the post oak trees as fast as his legs could carry him. It was nowhere near as swift as he wished. Riding so far and at such a pace was a very demanding and tiring business, even for a man who had spent much of his time on the back of a horse.

Perspiration flooded down the lieutenant's face and half blinded him. His breath, what little of it he could draw into his tortured lungs, was taken in brief, rasping gasps. Behind him, the sound of the horses' hooves came ever nearer as he continued to run. Each foot seemed to be growing heavier and more reluctant to follow the dictates of his will. With every stride it called for greater effort to make another. He knew the Lancers must be drawing close, but he had no way of telling exactly how far away they were. To look back would have been disastrous.

The grove, with its slender promise of safety and concealment, was still about fifty yards ahead when Dimmock's advancing left foot struck instead of passing over a small rock. Tripping, he stumbled on a few places vainly trying to recover his equilibrium. Failing to do so, he fell to the ground.

On the last occasion that the lieutenant had fallen, it had saved him from being killed. This latest mishap appeared to be evening up the balance. It was almost certain to cost him his life.

Something like a hundred yards away, the Mexicans saw Dimmock going down and they lowered the points of their lances forward and tucked the butts more firmly under their right elbows. Every one of them tried to urge his mount to go even faster so as to be the first to reach their prey.

❀   ❀   ❀   ❀   ❀

One of the first riders to be compelled to halt when Badillo's horse was shot, throwing the rider, was his sergeant major. The non-com had been at the rear of the advance guard, ensuring that the enlisted men did not forget their instructions and were far enough ahead of the Texians to prevent their mounts from being unduly frightened by the shooting. So he was leading the party as they returned to join in the killing. An experienced soldier, he had realized that a wild charge into the fray would be as great a hazard to the infantrymen as to the Texians and was setting a pace which would prevent it from happening.

Reining his mount at an angle and stopping it a scant two yards from Badillo, the sergeant major almost flung himself to the ground. He was about to bellow an order for the rest of the half troop to halt, but found that those nearest to him had already anticipated it. Leaping towards the major, he saw Dimmock galloping away. However, aware of the confusion that the sudden halt was causing, he did nothing about the Texian's departure. Nor did Refugio's shouted comment cause him to change his mind. His primary concern was for the safety of his superior, and that the other Lancers should be allowed to continue with their duties.

Bending down, the sergeant major turned Badillo over with surprising gentleness. He saw no sign of a wound, although he had not really expected to find one. The way in which the bay had collapsed suggested that it, and not its rider, had been shot.

Placing his hands beneath Badillo's armpits, the sergeant major turned and pulled him towards the left side of the trail. While doing so, the non-com glared up the slope, hoping to find out which of the infantryman had fired the shot. So many of them, including Sergeant Refugio, were reloading their rifles that it was impossible to tell who had been responsible for killing the bay.

'The major's not hurt bad!' the sergeant major informed the watching Lancers. 'Get going and kill some of those Texian bastards for him.'

Seeing what was happening, as he was replenishing

his rifle with powder and ball, Refugio did not know whether to be pleased or alarmed by the developments. The Lancers were resuming their interrupted advance and Badillo was lying in plain view and well clear of them. Against that, the sergeant major had not yet made any attempt to accompany them. Instead, he was kneeling and supporting the officer's shoulders with his bent leg. His presence at Badillo's side made the sergeant's unofficial task too dangerous to be contemplated.

Sergeant Major Gomez was noted throughout the Tamaulipa Brigade for his loyalty to Badillo. Being aware of the close bond between them, Refugio had no intention of making another attempt on the major's life. Gomez was one man with whom the sergeant had no intention of tangling. There were few men under Urrea's command, even the toughest hard-cases, who would have thought any the worse of Refugio if they had known of his sentiments.

To his face, Gomez's comrades-in-arms addressed him as 'Bravio', 'Ferocious', and 'Espantoso', meaning 'Fearful' or 'Terrible', any of which applied in full measure to his nature. They called him 'Yaqui' too, but only behind his back, and whispered stories of what had happened to a soldier who was foolish enough to make use of that nickname in his hearing.

Slightly over medium height, Gomez had a thickset body that bore not a surplus ounce of fat. On the few occasions when he allowed his hair to grow beyond its usual very close-cropped state, it was black and straight. This combined with his dark coppery-red features, high cheek-bones, slightly slanting brown eyes, a tight lipped mouth that rarely smiled and a broad, wide nostrilled nose was suggestive of Indian blood. Although his parentage was known, there were few who were unwise enough to mention it. Those who did never made the mistake a second time. He was as deadly and quick to kill as the man who sired him by raping his mother, a warrior of the tribe which gave him his third and least used sobriquet.

'Wha—What happened?' Badillo gasped, as his head cleared and he looked around. Seeing his men involved in the fighting, he tried to rise.

'Take it easy, sir,' Gomez advised, gently restraining the officer. 'One of these infantry bastards shot your horse and you took a bad fall. Is anything broken?'

'I don't think so,' Badillo decided, after moving his arms and legs. There was a certain amount of pain, but nothing to suggest that bones had been broken. 'Help me up and—'

'If you'll be advised by me, sir,' the sergeant major said politely, feeling the major swaying after he had obeyed the order. 'You'll stay here and let the men finish off the Texians.'

Much as Badillo would have like to become involved in the fighting, if only so that he could try to kill Saucedo, he could see the objections to it. He had sufficient respect for the fighting qualities of individual Texians (although he had small regard for them as an organized whole) to realize that he would need all his faculties working at their highest pitch in order to tangle with such desperate men. Still feeling the effects of being flung to the ground, he knew he would be unable to react with his customary speed.

'You're right,' the major conceded, weaving from side to side and feeling Gomez's arm tighten in support. 'I'd better sit down.'

Keeping an eye on the struggling mass of men and holding himself ready to defend Badillo if necessary, the sergeant major helped him to reach and sit on the dead horse's saddle. The officer turned his gaze to the wound in the animal's shoulder. Despite Gomez's earlier explanation, it was not until then that a full understanding of what had happened began to penetrate Badillo's head.

40

'Did you see who did this?' Badillo snarled, indicating the bullet hole.

'No,' Gomez confessed. 'By the time I looked, most of them were reloading.' Then, realizing what the question implied, he glared up the slope and went on, 'Do you think it might have been done deliberately?'

'I don't know,' the major replied, thinking about his own plans with regard to his rival. 'They are supposed to be the best shots in Saucedo's Battalion and a Baker's a damned accurate rifle.'

While Badillo was speaking, he stiffly and painfully twisted his torso and stared behind him. Standing protectively at his side, Gomez—who was armed with a sabre instead of a lance and had a pistol thrust into the opposite side of his weapon belt—also studied the slope. However, they had left it too late.

Refugio had noticed the sergeant major's earlier examination of the area and had taken warning from it. Discarding his notions of making a second attempt to earn his promotion, he had moved from his position. By the time he was once more under Gomez's observation, he was standing between the nearest pair of his men and staring at the fighting on the trail with unswerving attention.

'It could have been any of them,' Gomez growled, having forgotten where the sergeant had been the last time he looked. 'They all know that Saucedo hates your guts and would be pleased to see you dead.'

'Knowing it and trying to do something about it are two different things,' Badillo pointed out. 'There aren't many who'd think of it, or be willing to take a chance on doing it if they did. What kind of man is that sergeant?'

'Stupid, from what I've seen of him,' Gomez answered. 'But they say there's not a finer shot in the Battalion. I don't think he'd be smart enough to come up with the idea of killing you and making it look like it was accidental.'

'Saucedo could have told him to do it if he saw the chance,' the major countered, then swung an angry scowl towards the fighting. 'Damn it! If I could only get in among them—!'

'Nobody could blame you for not going, sir,' the sergeant major said soothingly, misunderstanding his superior's reason for wanting to participate. 'It was the fault of whoever shot your horse. Anyway, I don't think they're going to need our help to settle the Texians. So, if it's all right with you, I'll stay here. Just in case there might be more of them who've been told to do some "accidental" shooting.'

'Two pairs of eyes are better than one,' Badillo admitted. 'Go and fetch my sabre. I might need it if any of them should come this way.'

'Si, senor,' Gomez assented.

Keeping a watch on the men among the trees while the sergeant major went to collect his weapon, Badillo drew his pistol from the uppermost of his saddle's holsters. He noticed that, on completing their reloading, each of the riflemen gave their full attention to the fighting. Even the most logical suspect, Sergeant Refugio, made no attempt to turn his eyes in the major's direction.

'Gracias,' Badillo grunted, accepting the sabre with his left hand and spiking its point into the ground. Gesturing with the cocked pistol in his other fist, he continued, 'Having my horse shot was an understandable mistake. In a fight like that, *anybody* could be shot by "accident". I expect it's happened already and might again.'

'It might even happen to somebody as important as a colonel,' Gomez remarked, drawing and cocking his own pistol.

So, while the rest of their companions went on fighting, the major and his faithful subordinate remained where they were. They kept the tangle of human beings and horses under observation, with occasional glances to make sure that none of the men on the slopes were turning a weapon in Badillo's direction. But despite the pair's scrutiny of the battle, because Saucedo was always in the thickest of the fighting the chance to kill him did not present itself.

'Kill them!' the colonel bellowed, wild with blood lust, swinging his gore-smothered sword at a wounded Texian who was staggering past. The force of the blow almost removed the head from the body of the already dying man. 'Kill every last one of them.'

For all the desperate efforts of the Texians, the final outcome was inevitable. Rapidly outnumbered, unarmed apart from such weapons as they had been able to snatch from their assailants, within ten minutes the majority of them were either killed or dying.

Finally not one Texian remained on his feet in the valley. Breathing hard from their exertions, the Mexican soldiers were glaring around like fighting bulls who had smelled blood and sought further victims. Some of the more hard-bitten of them set about bayoneting or lancing any wounded that they found. Others, less callous and realizing for the first time exactly what they had been doing, stood silent. A few crossed themselves and took comfort in the thought that their Battalion's priests would grant them absolution and let them off with a minimal penance.

Despite all the Mexicans' precautions, several of the Texians had managed to break away from the fighting. Some were shot by the riflemen on the slopes. Others were ridden down and killed by the Lancers. However, there were those who were fortunate enough to avoid either fate. Of the latter, only Dimmock had contrived to obtain a horse. The remainder had fled on foot, making off through the woodland.

While self preservation might have been the basic motive behind most of the escapes, each of the fleeing

43

men had something else in mind. They wanted to spread the news of how Fannin's command had been betrayed and massacred at Goliad—and to see if there was any way in which revenge could be taken against the man who had ordered it to be carried out, General José Urrea.

CHAPTER FOUR
Kill Him Before They Reload!

ALTHOUGH Lieutenant Paul Dimmock managed to land on his hands and knees instead of sprawling flat to the ground, he knew that he could not hope to rise before his pursuers reached him.

Confident that they now had the Texian at their mercy, the six Mexicans were also relieved that the long and gruelling chase was almost over. But, foolishly, even though they knew they had left the area which the Tamaulipa Brigade had swept clear of all opposition, only one of them had eyes for anything other than their quarry.

'Look!' yelled the man with the badly scratched cheek, some instinct making him glance beyond their proposed victim. As a warning, the single word left much to be desired. It gave no indication of where he wanted to direct his companions' attention. Realizing its shortcomings, he supplemented it. 'Up there, by the trees!'

Catching the note of alarm in the Lancer's voice, the sergeant looked up. What he saw gave him as great a shock as it had the speaker.

Three armed men were running from the grove of post oaks.

Apparently they had emerged from concealment even before the Texian had fallen down, but had gone unnoticed by the Mexicans who had been too excited and engrossed in the prospect of catching and killing their victim.

Only one glance was needed for the sergeant to decide that the newcomers were unlikely to be friendly and had not come out of hiding to help capture, or kill, the man they were pursuing.

Two of the men were dressed in such a similar fashion that they might have been wearing some kind of uniform. Each had on a low-crowned, wide-brimmed black hat, a fringed buckskin shirt, a pair of tight fitting fawn riding breeches and black Hessian boots.* In addition to the rifles in their hands, both carried a pistol on the right side of the waistbelt and a massive, white handled knife—presumably of the kind already known, even to Mexicans, as a 'bowie', in honour of the man credited with designing the original weapon†—sheathed at the left. There was only one noticeable difference in the pair's attire. The taller and bulkier man's tightly rolled bandana was scarlet, while his companion sported one of a multi-hued riot of clashing colours.

In some ways, the third member of the party was even more remarkable than his companions. Much shorter, not more than five foot six, he was bare headed and had close cropped black hair. His face was an almond colour, with slanted eyes and cheerful features that did not appear to be either Mexican or Anglo-Saxon. A loose fitting black shirt hung outside somewhat baggy trousers of the same material which were tucked into Hessian boots. Unlike his companions, he had no firearms. Instead, a pair of long hilted, slightly curved swords—

---

* Hessian boots: riding boots originally designed for light cavalrymen such as Hussars. The legs came to just below the knee and had a 'V' notch in front.

† James Bowie was one of the defenders of the Alamo Mission. What happened to his knife, which was made by the Arkansas's blacksmith and master cutler, James Black, is told in: THE QUEST FOR BOWIE'S BLADE.

the one on the right being some inches shorter than its mate at the left—swung from slings attached to his leather waist belt. He held a six foot long bow with an arrow nocked to its string. If the Mexicans had been more observant, they might have noticed that its handle was set two thirds of the way down the stave instead of centrally. There was a quiver suspended across his back, so that the flights of the arrows it held rose over his right shoulder and were readily accessible to his 'draw' hand.

Despite the rifles held by the two taller of the newcomers, the sergeant and his party felt little anxiety. In fact, the alarm in the voice of the man with the scratched face had been caused more by surprise than fear. Nothing they had seen of Texians so far, either at San Patricio or Goliad, had led them to form a healthy respect for the rebels' fighting qualities. At neither place had they shown to any great advantage.

There was something that the Lancers were failing to take into account. At San Patricio, the men opposing them had been an undisciplined and disaffected rabble who were the remains of the force with which—against Houston's orders—the adventurer, Colonel Frank Johnson, had planned to attack and loot Matamoros. The troops at Goliad had already lost all faith in their commanding officer and were demoralized *before* they had been surrounded by the vastly superior numbers of the Tamaulipa Brigade.

If the six Mexicans had fought at San Antonio de Bexar, either in December the previous year* or during

* On December the 11th, 1835, General Martin Perfecto Cós and eleven hundred Mexican soldiers were defeated and compelled to surrender at San Antonio de Bexar by Colonels Milam and Bureleson's much smaller force. On giving his parole that he and his men would not participate in any further military activity against the Texians, they were all released and allowed to return to Mexico. Cós did not keep his word and subsequently returned to take part in the siege of the Alamo Mission.

46

the siege of the Alamo Mission, they would not have been so disdainful of Texians' fighting prowess.

Nor did the Lancers consider that the three men would be able to prevent them from killing the Texian. Even though they had the greater distance to cover before reaching him, their horses were carrying them much faster than the trio could run.

The same thought obviously occurred to the newcomers. However, their solution to the problem did not appeal to be the wisest to the racing Mexicans. But, it was what the Lancers expected of Texians.

Coming to a halt, the two taller men raised their rifles. The other, strange looking, man, clearly considering that he was at a distance where his weapon would not prove effective, continued to advance. However, he took care not to come between his companions and the Lancers.

Having sighted, the two men squeezed their triggers practically in unison. Flame and white smoke lunged from the muzzles of the rifles. Back snapped the head of the Mexican who had drawn ahead of his companions and his *shako* spun upwards from it. Letting his lance drop, he slid limply from his saddle and followed the weapon to the ground. Although the sergeant had also been singled out for attention, he was more fortunate. He too lost his headdress, the bullet merely removed it by striking the badge and not ripping through his skull.

A hard-bitten veteran, the non-com was still startled by the narrow escape. Involuntarily he drew back on his horse's reins with a snatch that caused it to slacken its already leg-weary gait. The pause allowed his companions to draw ahead of him. However, he recovered his nerve quickly enough and encouraged his mount to increase its speed. Studying the two newcomers, he concluded that the worst of the danger was over. The rifles were now empty and there was no time for them to be made ready for use again. In all probability, the men would drop them and try to continue the fight with the pistols. To his way of thinking, the handguns posed much less of a threat than the rifles.

'Keep going!' the sergeant bellowed, noticing that some of his Lancers were looking back at him and showing signs of perturbation. 'We can kill him before they reload.'

Raising his head as he heard the shots, Dimmock stared at his rescuers through eyes half blinded by sweat. What he saw caused him to experience a momentary surge of relief. Not only did he recognize the two men's attire as that of the Texas Light Cavalry, but he felt sure that he could name both of them.

Six foot tall, the man on the right was heavily built and conveyed an impression of well padded lethargy. Curly, auburn hair showed from beneath his hat. Despite the gravity of the situation, his sun-reddened features retained something of an amiable and almost sleepy expression. Unless Dimmock was mistaken, his name was Mannen Blaze.

Matching his companion in height, the second man's straight-backed, whipcord lean frame—set off to its best advantage by the well tailored garments—made him appear slightly shorter. He had black hair, but it was his face that supplied the clue to his identity. Brows like inverted 'V's' over coal black eyes, an aquiline nose, a neatly trimmed moustache and a short, sharp pointed chin beard gave the features an almost Satanic cast which, in part, accounted for why Captain Jackson Baines Hardin was nicknamed 'Ole Devil'.*

As the third member of the rescue party was advancing outside the lieutenant's range of vision, which was restricted by perspiration and exhaustion, the two young

---

* Another reason for the sobriquet was his reputation for being a 'lil ole devil' in a fight.

men—neither had yet reached twenty-six years of age—appeared to be alone and to have no other assistance.

Nor did they seem to have a very clear grasp of the situation!

The smoke that was still curling away from the muzzles proved that each of the newcomers had fired his *single barrelled* rifle. So Dimmock duplicated the Mexican sergeant's line of reasoning on what they would do next.

Much to the lieutenant's consternation, the pair made no attempt to do either of the things which he and the non-com were anticipating.

It was almost as if Dimmock's would-be rescuers were unaware that they now held empty weapons. They neither dropped the rifles as a prelude to drawing their pistols, nor lowered the butts in preparation to start reloading.

Dimmock found the pair's lack of activity puzzling to say the least. Although he had never met them, he knew something of Ole Devil Hardin and Mannen Blaze. They had already begun to earn themselves reputations for being fighting men of the first water. It was said that they were courageous without being reckless, over-confident or foolhardy and possessed considerable knowledge where the handling of weapons was concerned. In the latter case particularly, the lieutenant felt that they were not living up to their reputations. He wondered if, having rushed into their present predicament without taking the odds against them into account, they were now frozen into immobility with fright.

If Dimmock had been less exhausted and emotionally disturbed, he might have noticed certain things about the two Texians' weapons; although, even if he had, it was improbable he would have appreciated what it meant. At first glance, the rifles which were still at their shoulders seemed to be ordinary enough. However, even a casual closer look would have disclosed a few small differences and one major one. Not only did Dimmock fail to detect the unusual aspects, but certain small movements being made by his rescuers also escaped his observation.

The sergeant and the four remaining Lancers were no better informed, nor more observant. They were still too far away to see the less obvious aspects of what was happening. Even if they had been closer, they too were unlikely to have appreciated the point of the Texians' right thumbs manipulating a small lever on the side of their rifles' frame.

Keener sighted than his companions, the sergeant noticed that the pair's right forefingers emerged from the triggerguards, went forward to cock the hammer—which was below the frame instead of, as was more usual, on top—and returned to their original positions. However, he failed to see what the actions had achieved as the rifles had already been fired once and had not yet been reloaded. To the sergeant's way of thinking, small though he might be, the third member of the rescue party could pose a much greater threat than either of his larger companions. At least he had a weapon that was capable of being discharged almost immediately.

Having advanced a further half a dozen strides, the third of the party came to a halt. Standing erect, with his torso turned sideways to the direction of his spread apart feet, he raised the bow to the perpendicular. Then he began to draw it in a manner that was unlike anything the sergeant had ever seen, even though he had fought against Indian archers on several occasions in Mexico and was sufficiently impressed by their capabilities to have studied their methods.*

That was, although the non-com had no way of knowing, only to be expected. Some people thought that

* *A more detailed description of the Japanese techniques and an explanation of how Tommy Okasi arrived in the United States is given in: YOUNG OLE DEVIL.*

50

Tommy Okasi was Chinese. In fact, he came from the—at that time*—virtually unknown Japanese islands and was well trained in all his nation's very effective martial arts. The Japanese archery techniques differed in some respects from those commonly known, such as the position of the handle on the stave† and the way of making the draw.**

Deeply alarmed by what he regarded as Ole Devil Hardin's and Mannen Blaze's stupidity, Dimmock tried to yell some kind of abusive advice at them. With his lungs so depleted of air, the words would not come. Nor, as they were engrossed in taking sight along the barrels of their empty and useless rifles, could they see the distress and torment on his face.

Rage and frustration tore at the lieutenant. Once he was dead, even if the pair of would-be rescuers survived, they would not learn of the massacre at Goliad. So his desertion of his comrades-in-arms would have been in vain.

Even as Dimmock was struggling to register his feelings vocally, he saw the two men's forefingers tightening on the triggers.

Up flipped the under-hammers!

While the Mexicans were still too far away to see as much as their proposed victim could, they soon found out. Once again, although it was impossible as far as their knowledge went, the rifles cracked and spat out lead with deadly effect.

Struck between the eyes, the man with the scratched

There was no large scale contact between Japan and the Western World until the visits made by a flotilla of the United States' Navy under the command of Commodore Perry in 1853-54.

†*The off-set position of the handle was to allow men of small stature to wield such lengthy bows.*

**Two occidental styles of handling a bow are described in:* BUNDUKI.

cheek was killed outright and never knew of the phenomenon. Almost at the same instant, one of the bareheaded riders lost more than the *shako* which had been swept from him while following Dimmock through the woodland. A bullet struck him in the centre of the throat and slammed him, spurting blood from the torn open jugular vein, backwards off of his horse. Hissing through the air faster than the eye could follow, the arrow loosed by Tommy Okasi impaled the left breast of the second man to have lost his headdress. Although he did not fall from his mount immediately, the lance slipped from his grasp and he involuntarily reined the animal away to the right before death claimed him and he toppled to the ground.

Once again, pure chance had kept the sergeant alive. So swiftly had everything happened that he still had not regained the ground lost when the shock of nearly being shot had caused him to slow down. The three victims had been ahead of him and had taken the brunt of the attack.

It was more than just the sight of his three companions being killed that caused the last of the Lancers to lose his nerve. Like all of his party, he had believed that the Texians were holding empty rifles. Discovering that they were able to fire a second time without reloading, in some way which he could not understand, he was filled with superstitious dread. Wishing that he had a free hand to cross himself and ward off what he felt sure must be evil spirits, he swung his horse to the left. It was his intention to flee before one of the magical weapons was turned in his direction.

Conscious of his last companion's desertion, the sergeant was made of sterner stuff. Having come so far, he meant to finish what he had set out to do. He had no more idea than the Lancer of how empty rifles were able to deal out death to two more of his men, but he refused to let that sway him from his purpose. Ignoring the two

Texians, who were still lining the weapons, he aimed his lance at the back of his kneeling victim.

The second shots had surprised Dimmock just as much as the Mexicans. For a moment, he thought that his rescuers must be using double barrelled rifles. Then he realized that was not the answer. Each weapon had but a single barrel.

Surprise and puzzlement caused the lieutenant to forget his deadly peril. Staring at the rifle in Ole Devil Hardin's hands, he noticed that it was different in at least two respects from the more conventional arms with which he was familiar. In the first place, no provision had been made for carrying a ramrod suspended below the octagonal barrel where it would be readily accessible for reloading. If he had been able to see he would have noticed that. Although the position of the hammer —which the satanic-faced Texian's forefinger was once again drawing to full cock—was not common, it had been utilized by more than one gunsmith.

The most important and significant departure from normal was a rectangular metal bar with rounded ends which passed through the rifle's frame above where the head of the hammer would strike when released. There were holes drilled into the face of the bar. Dimmock noticed that the three on the right were apparently plugged with grease, but the one at the left was clear yet blackened like the muzzle of a pistol when a shot had been fired through it.

Even as Dimmock became aware of the bar, it began to move, seemingly of its own volition. Creeping to the left, it exposed a second empty and powder blackened hole and one of those which were blocked with grease disappeared into the frame. He could not make out exactly what had happened, or why.

The lieutenant's lack of comprehension was understandable. There were comparatively few people in Texas, or the United States for that matter, who would have recognized and been aware of the full potential of Ole Devil Hardin's and Mannen Blaze's weapons. They were, in fact, a fairly successful attempt by the Mormon gunsmith, Jonathan Browning, to produce an arm capable of firing more than one shot without the need to reload in the conventional manner.

Despite the difficulty of transporting it with the magazine in place, Browning had developed a rifle capable of continuous fire unequalled by contemporary weapons.* The metal bar was, in fact a five shot magazine; this having been the number he had considered most suitable for convenient handling. After a bullet had been discharged, operating the lever with the right thumb caused the magazine to pass through the aperture in the receiver until the next loaded chamber was in position. Then the mechanism thrust the magazine forward to make a gas-tight seal against the bore of the barrel and locked it firmly. As a further aid to operation, the proximity of the under-hammer to the right forefinger permitted it to be cocked without the need to remove the butt from the shoulder.

With the mechanisms of the rifles operating, Ole Devil and his cousin realized that the next loaded chambers would not be in place sufficiently quickly to stop the sergeant. Already he was very close to the man on the ground and he showed no sign of turning aside from the threat of their weapons.

Tommy Okasi was equally aware of the danger and just as helpless to avert it. After loosing the arrow, his right hand had flashed upwards and was drawing

---

* For all the Browning Slide Repeating rifle's advantages, it never achieved the fame it deserved. During the period when he was manufacturing it, between 1834 and '42, he lacked the facilities for large scale production. In later years when he would have been able to do so, the development of metallic cartridges and more compact, if less simple, repeating arms had made it obsolete.

another shaft from the quiver. Swiftly as he was acting, he would not have time to nock it to the string, make his draw, sight and release it in time to stop the Mexican killing the man they were trying to save.

Suddenly the rapidly approaching thunder of hooves recalled Dimmock to a remembrance of his situation. A glance to his rear showed him just how grave it still was. The sergeant's horse was so close that it seemed to loom right above him and the head of the lance was rushing with terrifying speed towards the centre of his back.

Self preservation, that strongest of human emotions, caused Dimmock to react without the need for conscious thought. He threw himself to the right in a desperate rolling motion—and not a moment too soon!

The lance's head missed its mark by such a narrow margin that the lieutenant felt it scrape lightly across his back before spiking into the ground.

Realizing that his weapon had missed its intended target, the sergeant allowed it to turn and plucked its head free. He was swinging it forward, hoping to take one of the Texians with him, when both of the rifles roared and hurled bullets up into his body. Almost as soon as the loads had been expelled through the forty and five-sixteenths inch long barrels, Ole Devil and Mannen sprang aside, allowing the horse to carry its dying rider between them.

Having set up his bow, Tommy saw it would not be needed to help deal with the sergeant. So he pivoted and, after taking aim, sent his arrow through the back of the fleeing Lancer.

Finishing his evasion action face down, Dimmock lay sobbing for breath, full of relief at his deliverance from what had appeared to be certain death.

Lowering the Browning rifle, Ole Devil looked at the lieutenant and identified the uniform of the Brazos Guards. However, he gave a quick and negative shake of his head when Mannen Blaze was on the point of advancing. Despite his general air of lethargy, the burly red head was anything but the slow witted dullard he liked to appear. Realizing why his cousin had made the prohibitive gesture, he too stood still. They waited until Dimmock had recovered something of his composure before advancing to hear his news.

CHAPTER FIVE
They'll Have To Go Unavenged

SITTING at an ancient, rickety, collapsible table in the large 'umbrella' type tent which was serving as his temporary office and headquarters, Major General Samuel Houston listened to the conclusion of Lieutenant Paul Dimmock's report on the massacre of Colonel James W. Fannin's command at Goliad. Then he slowly swung his gaze to where Captain Jackson Baines Hardin was standing, ramrod straight, despite having received permission to be 'at ease'.

Ole Devil returned the scrutiny, trying to ascertain from the General's Indian-dark face how he was taking the news that close to four hundred Texians had been murdered in cold blood. As on a previous occasion, when the young captain had attempted to deduce how Houston regarded some of his apparently irresponsible —although actually justifiable under the circumstances —activities, he learned nothing from the grimly impassive features. For all that, Ole Devil realized the information must have come as a terrible shock.

More than any other person—even Governor David G. Burnet, Lieutenant Governor James W. Robinson, or any other member of the Provisional Government that had been assembled and elected at Washington-on-the-

Brazos on March the 2nd, 1836—Sam Houston held the responsibility for the future of the Republic of Texas in his hands.

Appointed to command the hastily recruited Army, Houston had found himself leading what was for the most part a horde of rugged individualists. Capable fighters, highly skilled in handling weapons of various kinds, such men had only the slightest idea of accepting discipline and even less about the value of co-operative and co-ordinated efforts for the common good. Some of the senior officers, Colonels Fannin and Frank Johnson for example, had been blatant opportunists who were more concerned with schemes for their personal aggrandizement and profit than in conforming to a sensible strategic policy. Others had been made over confident by the previous year's successes at San Antonio, Gonzales, and other sites of action where the Mexicans had been defeated without difficulty; failing to realize that these had been against inferior troops and that the real tests were still to come.

Houston had a better understanding of the situation and had planned his strategy accordingly.

What the General set out to do did not meet with everybody's approval. He had ordered a withdrawal to the east instead of attempting to make an immediate stand. At their own insistence, Colonels William Barrett Travis, James Bowie and Davey Crockett had remained at the Alamo Mission with less than two hundred volunteers. They had promised to hold their ground and gain time in which the General could build up a force capable of meeting *Presidente* Antonio Lopez de Santa Anna's army in open conflict with some hope of success.

Persuading the Texians, particularly those whose homes and businesses were in the west, to retire from the scene of battle had not been easy. While it had been achieved, Houston was compelled by the weight of adverse public opinion to abandon his militarily sound idea of laying

57

waste to the country as they left it. To have done so would have increased Santa Anna's already difficult task of feeding and supplying the other needs of his army.

The news of the Alamo's fall, with what was believed to have been the death of every defender,* had come as a not unexpected yet still deeply disturbing and alarming blow. Nor had morale been improved by what was already being referred to as the 'Runaway Scrape', when —on March the 18th, 1836—despite the nearest enemy being many miles away, the members of the Provisional Government had deserted Washington-on-the-Brazos. They had fled eastwards with, so they claimed, the intention of establishing a 'temporary capital' at the small town of Harrisburg.

It had taken the full force of Houston's personality and the backing of his most loyal supporters to hold together the main body of the Army when the news of the Government's flight had been received. To do so had called for a concession on the General's part. Many of the men had only remained because there seemed to be a chance of imminent and more positive action than withdrawal.

Having learned that there was much bitterness and dissension among Santa Anna's force because of their heavy losses during the thirteen days' siege of the Alamo Mission, Houston had reluctantly agreed to make a stand on the eastern bank of the Colorado River. However, he had warned his men that they would have to have Fannin's assistance if they were to succeed. The colonel had the largest, best equipped and, arguably, finest trained single outfit in the Republic of Texas's Army and their numbers might easily spell the difference between victory or defeat. Accordingly, Houston had sent orders for Fannin to destroy Fort Defiance—as his

* Recent research suggests that one of the defenders, Brigido Guerrero, escaped death by convincing his captors that he was a loyal Mexican who had been held prisoner by the Texians.

well defended base at Goliad had been named by a popular ballot of its then enthusiastic garrison—and join the rest of the Army at their camp on the Colorado River.

Days had slipped by without the Mexicans putting in an appearance, but neither did Fannin and his men. So Houston had sent Ole Devil, who had recently brought another important mission to a successful conclusion, to find out what was delaying them.

Seeing Dimmock heading in their direction and being chased by the Lancers, Ole Devil and his two companions had made ready to rescue him. Leaving their horses concealed in the post oaks' grove, they had waited at its edge in the hope that he would lead his pursuers to them. The failure of his horse to keep going had caused them to take action sooner than they had anticipated, but the unexpected qualities of the Browning Slide Repeating rifles and Tommy Okasi's archery had saved the lieutenant's life.

On learning of the massacre, Ole Devil had told his companions to range in the direction of Goliad and watch for any other members of Fannin's ill-fated command who might have escaped. Then he had caught a couple of the dead Mexicans' horses. After allowing the animals to rest and recover as far as possible from the strain of the chase, he had set off with Dimmock to report to the General. Riding relay, as he, Mannen Blaze and Tommy Okasi had been doing when they had first seen the pursuit, the two young men had reached the camp on the Colorado River during the late afternoon of March the 28th.

Their arrival had aroused considerable interest, but Ole Devil had managed to avoid answering the many questions which had been thrown at them. The lieutenant's dishevelled appearance and haggard, woeful attitude had been excused on the grounds of his having ridden from Goliad at high speed, but his reason for having done so was not mentioned. Fortunately, the unofficial interrogation had not been prolonged. Hearing that they had come and sensing that something must be seriously wrong, Houston had wasted no time in having them brought to him. In addition, he had insisted that the interview be held in the privacy of his quarters and with nobody else present.

'So Fannin's damned incom—Fannin and his whole command have been killed,' Houston said, half to himself, stopping just in time from giving a bitter condemnation of the dead colonel. 'Almost four hundred men butchered without a chance.'

'I—I didn't run because I was afraid, sir,' Dimmock declared hastily, as the General's blue eyes—which were strangely young looking in such a seamed and leathery face—returned to him.

'Any man who says you did is a liar and a fool, mister,' Houston replied, studying the lieutenant's drooping posture. It was redolent of exhaustion and deep distress in case his motives should have been misinterpreted. 'And anyone who says so in my hearing will wish he'd been born deaf and dumb as well as stupid.'

Listening to the softly spoken, yet vibrant words, Ole Devil could see how much they had been appreciated by Dimmock. There was nothing in them to show how deeply the news had affected Houston, despite it having been such a serious blow to his plans for the future. A lesser man might have taken out his disappointment on the bearer of the bad tidings, but that was not the General's way. From the beginning, he had shown a sympathy which had done much to draw out the lieutenant's hesitant story of the massacre. It was an example which Ole Devil would remember and put to use in later years, when he found himself holding a high military rank under difficult conditions.*

---

* *One such occasion is recorded in*: THE DEVIL GUN.

'It's possible there were other survivors, sir,' Ole Devil commented, wanting to help relieve Dimmock's anxieties as there were further details that needed explaining, one of which was what had happened at Goliad prior to the garrison being marched out to its death. 'We only waited for about two hours, which didn't give Cousin Mannen and Tommy much time to find them and rejoin us. Mr. Dimmock wanted to stay longer, but I considered his information was too important to be delayed.'

'You were right in that,' Houston confirmed, nodding his white haired head approvingly. He could see that Dimmock was relieved at having been exonerated of any desire to continue his flight without considering the possibility of other survivors. The comment was clear proof that the Mephistophelian-featured young captain had a keen grasp of the situation and considerable knowledge of human nature. 'Please God there were others who escaped, but for you to have waited wouldn't have helped them. You've done more good by getting here as quickly as possible.'

'Thank you, sir,' Dimmock said gratefully.

'Was the destruction of Fort Defiance carried out?' the General went on.

'Yes, sir,' the lieutenant replied. 'We blew the trunnions off the cannon, as we'd no means of hauling them, and threw the shot into the San Antonio River before we left.'

'Do you know anything about the military chest containing the pay for the troops?' Houston inquired, hoping that in some way the not inconsiderable sum of money—close to ten thousand dollars in United States' silver and gold coins—had not been allowed to fall into the Mexican's hands.

'Colonel Fannin had it buried and the spot hidden when we were surrounded, sir.' Dimmock answered and his face darkened with anger. 'Then it was dug up to purchase our release. God damn it! It was supposed to ensure our safety!'

At that moment, before the lieutenant could continue with his tirade, a voice from outside the tent asked if it would be all right to enter. On receiving permission, a sombre-faced colonel walked in.

'This young man's arrival has caused a lot of unrest among the men, sir,' the colonel stated, darting a look at Dimmock's angry face. 'Would it be possible to tell them when we can expect Fannin to get here?'

'Fannin won't be coming, Jack,' Houston answered quietly, then gave a shrug. 'Have assembly blown. It's no use keeping what's happened from them.'

'Yes, sir,' the colonel replied, his gaze flickering from the General to Dimmock and back. He paused for a moment as if meaning to ask another question, thought better of it and turned, saying, 'I'll have it done straight away.'

'Go and try to get some rest, Mr. Dimmock,' Houston ordered, after the colonel had left. 'I know it won't be easy, but I can assure you that you've nothing to reproach yourself over. Without your information, we'd have waited in vain for Fannin to come. Now I can avoid any delay in taking action.'

'Can I ask what that action will be, sir?' Ole Devil inquired, although he could guess at the answer.

'There's no chance of us making a stand here now,' Houston replied. 'And I think that the men will see that when I tell them what happened to Fannin's command. We'll resume our withdrawal to the east in the morning.'

'Is there any way we can get revenge, or make the Mexicans pay for what they've done, sir?' Dimmock demanded angrily.

'Not at the moment, much as I wish there was,' Houston admitted. 'Many of the men with Fannin were my friends. But I'm afraid they'll have to go unavenged for now.'

And for all time, Ole Devil thought, unless the Texians defeated Santa Anna's army—which did not seem likely to happen under the circumstances. In fact, as things stood at that moment, there was a very good chance that the men who were responsible for the massacre would never be brought to account for their crimes.

*   *   *   *   *

Even as Houston was making his pronouncement, the man who had been behind the decision to wipe out Fannin's command was looking at the two officers who had been assigned to carry it out.

If fear of retribution, or twinges of conscience were troubling General José Urrea, he showed no sign of it. A big man, just topping the six foot level, he had the look of a formerly muscular and very active soldier whose present lack of exercise was causing him to run to fat. He was swarthily handsome, but the signs of too much easy living and dissipation were starting to leave their traces. What was more, his attempts to plaster the remains of once luxuriant black hair over a bare patch on the top of his head could not entirely hide the fact that he was going bald. For all that, with the aid of a corset, he still filled his costly and perfectly tailored uniform in a way that he felt sure was most appealing to members of the opposite sex.

On the arrival of the Tamaulipa Brigade in Goliad, Urrea had taken over the best house in the town for his headquarters. Seated in its owner's well furnished study, he hoisted a black Napoleon leg boot* on to the top of the desk and scratched the smooth, polished surface with an angry motion of a sharp rowelled spur. The action did not go unnoticed by the other three occu-

---

* Napoleon leg boot: one of knee length, the top higher at the front than the back, as frequently worn by Napoleon Bonaparte.

pants of the room. Two of them did not care for what it implied. They knew the General had the kind of nature that took a childish delight in such senseless acts of vandalism, particularly when something was displeasing him.

Urrea's attitude was puzzling to Colonel Sebastian Saucedo and Major Carlos Badillo. Taken all in all, he ought to have been satisfied by the way in which his part of the campaign against the Texian rebels was progressing. Unlike the main body of the Mexican Army, which had been reduced by close to a thousand dead and at least as many wounded during the fighting at the Alamo Mission, the Tamaulipa Brigade could consider themselves very fortunate in the matter of casualties. Against the few of his men who had been killed or injured could be balanced two successful engagements and the removal of several burdensome prisoners. In addition, there had been the gathering of much loot.

Although the two officers did not know it, the latter consideration was the cause of the General's annoyance.

'According to my figures, gentlemen,' announced the dry-as-dust voice of the man who was standing at the right of Urrea's chair consulting a sheet of paper in his hand, 'twenty-seven of the Texians are still to be accounted for.'

To many people, Major Francisco Alvarez seemed to exist solely for the purpose of gathering numbers and producing statistics. The fascination which he showed for such dull matters far exceeded the requirements of his position as Paymaster to the Tamaulipa Brigade. Statistics were apparently, his only interest in life. Although he wore the uniform of a regular army officer, his stoop-shouldered, lanky build and habit of peering short-sightedly through a pair of steel-rimmed glasses made him look more of a bookkeeper or clerk than a soldier. His manner of speaking was pompous and his aesthetic features were marred by lips which never smiled. Nothing appeared to strike him as humorous and he exuded an aura of solemn disapproval which most people with whom he came into contact found either irritating or infuriating.

'*My* men did their part, general!' Saucedo growled, bristling with the indignation which always came when he thought he was being made the target of criticism. He paused, darted a defiant glance at Badillo and waited for comment. When none came he continued with his exculpatory explanation. 'There were too many of them breaking away for the sharpshooters I'd put on the slope to be able to deal with them all. It takes time to reload a rifle. Damn it, if the Lancers had done what they were supposed to—.'

'They did,' Badillo interrupted, oozing icy politeness. 'It was *your* suggestion that all of my troop came back to help with the fighting.'

'We should have had some more of them hidden on the slopes,' Saucedo declared.

'To have done so would have increased the chances of the Texians spotting the ambush,' Badillo pointed out, determined that his regiment should not be held responsible for the escapes. 'I warned you what might happen.'

'I can't see why we had to set up an ambush,' Saucedo grumbled. 'It would have been easier and more efficient to shoot them where we were holding them instead of waiting until they were in the woodland.'

'*Presidente* Santa Anna didn't want it done that way,' Alvarez replied in a dispassionate tone. 'He wanted to avoid the story of what happened reaching the United States. That is why we couldn't take the more certain way out.'

As always, when watching or listening to the Paymaster, Badillo found himself wondering how a beautiful woman like Beatriz could have taken such a dull and unattractive man for a husband. Not, the cavalry major reminded himself cheerfully, that she had paid any great attention to her marriage vows when in *his* company.

'Damn it, I did *my* best!' Saucedo bellowed. 'it's all very well for you to stand there waving a sheet of paper—.'

'I'm merely giving the report that General Urrea asked for, colonel,' Alvarez answered, with calm disinterest. 'According to my orders, I have checked the number of dead against the total who left here and there is a discrepancy. All of the search parties have returned—.'

'Not *all* of them,' Badillo corrected. 'Six of my men went after one who got away on a horse. They have not come back yet.'

'Let's hope they're more use than some of you were!' Saucedo spat out.

'If my horse hadn't been shot—!' Badillo began, just as heatedly.

'Now, gentlemen,' Urrea put in, swinging his foot to the floor and slapping the desk top with the palm of his right hand. 'Despite Francisco's figures, I don't think things went off too badly. Your organization was good and you both played your parts very well. Anyway, no matter what *el Presidente* wants, it won't do any harm if the ones who get away spread the word of what's happened to the rest of that Texian scum. In fact, it's likely to scare them back into the United States.'

While the General overtly encouraged the rivalry between the two most powerful and influential officers under his command, he had no desire to see it come to a head. By keeping them both alive, he prevented either from growing strong enough to threaten his position. He had ambitious plans for the future in which they would both be needed to play a part. That was why he had intervened, as he had the previous afternoon, to avert a clash that might result in the death of one of them.

The trouble had almost come to a head on the trail

after the fighting had ended. Furious over his narrow escape and also because of his suspicions, Badillo had come close to provoking the kind of incident the General was anxious to avoid. He had been on the point of confronting Saucedo, who had made a disparaging comment about him having taken no part in the struggle, when Urrea and Alvarez—the General's ever present shadow—had arrived. Learning the cause of the disagreement, Urrea had—with the Paymaster's assistance—managed to calm down both officers. To prevent further trouble from erupting, Alvarez had suggested that the hunting of such Texians as had escaped should be organized. This had ensured that the colonel and the major were kept out of each other's company. However, the General knew that their animosity was still as strong as ever. Nor would he have had it any other way.

Searching for the escapees had occupied Saucedo and Badillo for most of the next twenty-four hours. As Alvarez's figures proved, their efforts had not been entirely successful. However, the colonel had used some of the time to his own advantage. He knew that the major guessed the shooting of his horse had been the result of an attempt to murder him, and he had taken steps to prevent him from learning the truth. Accompanying Sergeant Refugio, ostensibly to hunt for one of the Texians, the colonel had contrived to knock him over a cliff so that he fell unconscious into the San Antonio River and was drowned. There had been no witnesses and, although Badillo suspected what had happened, he had been unable to prove the sergeant's death was anything but an accident.

The summons to report to Urrea's office was not, as Saucedo and Badillo imagined, merely to let them know how many of the Texians had avoided being killed. They were there so that the General could try to find out what they knew of the ransom Fannin had paid to secure the release of his men.

The money and not orders from Santa Anna (whose dispatch merely requested that the prisoners be disposed of in whatever way might prove most convenient) had been why Urrea had insisted on them being killed in such a manner. If he had placed them in front of formal firing squads, there could have been a danger that some mention of the ransom would have been made. *El Presidente* had spies in the Tamaulipa Brigade and the General had no desire to turn over even part of the ransom money to him. In fact, Urrea intended to use it to finance his bid to overthrow Santa Anna and become the ruler of Mexico.

Nor was Urrea's display of annoyance caused by the information reported by Alvarez. He was irritated at having to spend time questioning the two officers when there were more enjoyable matters awaiting his attention. Although he would have preferred that all the Texians were killed, he was not unduly worried over the few who had escaped. Fannin's insistence upon secrecy when making the offer had implied that he did not want his men to learn how he had secured their release. So it was probable that he had not told them.* In which case, it was possible that none of the survivors were aware of what had happened to the money. Certainly they would not know that Urrea and Alvarez had collected it on Friday night, before offering the parole the next morning.

After Alvarez had asked sufficient questions to satisfy him that neither the colonel nor the major had heard about the ransom, Urrea told them there was to be a celebration that night. While the enlisted men held a *fiesta* in the town's *plaza*, the officers were to attend a ball at which the beautiful and gracious *Senora* Beatriz

---

* *Fannin had not intended to mention the ransom, but was compelled to do so as the other officers were suspicious of Urrea's motives in offering to accept their parole.*

Alvarez was to be hostess. Watching them leave, the General felt contented. The promise of the festivities had caused them to forget their differences for the time being and he would not have that to trouble him.

More important, they had not learned of the money that he had acquired to help his plans for the future. In addition, according to the latest reports, Santa Anna was once more on the march. Soon the Texians would be driven out and there would be no repercussions over the killing of the three hundred and seventy-three prisoners.

Thinking of the last two points, Urrea felt a sense of satisfaction. He had guessed why Houston was withdrawing to the east and knew that there would soon be a confrontation. Unless he was mistaken, it would be a hard and bloody battle and that was what he wanted. He had a plan in mind that would ensure that the Tamaulipa Brigade remained at its present strength no matter how many more men Santa Anna lost in quelling the rebellion. So Urrea would be able to fall upon the weakened *el Presidente* with a greater chance of success.

The ball that evening would allow the General to make his intentions known and to set them in motion.

CHAPTER SIX
It Could Mean Certain Death

WITH the burly man's arms encircling his waist, Ole Devil Hardin was raised from the ground and thrust against the trunk of a fair sized white ash tree. He grunted involuntarily. Not only were his ribs being crushed in a painful manner, but his back was forced against the rough, interlacing ridges and fissures of the greyish bark and his buckskin shirt offered only minimal protection.

Depending on their sympathies, the watching crowd let out exclamations of alarm or showed their satisfaction. While the fight had been fast paced and hectic, with most of the punishment going to Ole Devil's larger and heavier opponent, the spectators now considered that it was as good as over. Previously, the young captain's speed, matched by a knowledge of the French foot boxing known as *savate* and some mighty slick wrestling tricks, had allowed him to more than hold his own. However, having been brought to such close quarters put him at a serious disadvantage. His assailant had a well deserved reputation for strength and roughhouse brawling. The bear hug was one of the burly, buckskin clad man's pet tactics and had brought him victory on several occasions.

Holding his cousin's hat, percussion fired .54 calibre Manton* single barrel pistol, and ivory handled James Black bowie knife, Mannen Blaze looked on with some concern. He wondered if for once Ole Devil might have taken on too big a chore. However, he realized that there was nothing he could do to help. If he attempted to intervene, so would the burly man's supporters and that might bring the whole of the crowd into the fight.

Standing at Mannen's side, Tommy Okasi looked different from when he had helped to save Lieutenant Paul Dimmock's life.† While his clothing and armament were the same, (except that he had left off the quiver of arrows,) he had not yet removed all of the disguise which he had adopted to carry out a dangerous assign-

---

* *Joseph 'Old Joe' Manton, a gunsmith of London, England, who was an early maker of top quality pistols and rifles employing the percussion fired mechanism.*

† *Lieutenant Dimmock was later killed while helping to raid Santa Anna's column as it followed the retreating Republic of Texas's Army.*

ment two nights earlier.* So his skin still retained the dark brown colour produced by a stain which he had manufactured.† The result was remarkable. He lacked the characteristic 'hawk' nose, but the effect of the curious trait known as the 'shovel incisor'—in which the inner surfaces of the upper front teeth are concave, as though scooped out—combined with the fleshy eyelids and folds that gave his eyes their slanted appearance made him seem more Indian than Oriental. It had been even more pronounced when he had been dressed suitably and had worn a black wig that had been supplied by a member of a small theatrical troupe who had been entertaining the Republic of Texas's Army.

Like Mannen, Tommy was studying Ole Devil's predicament. He was less perturbed by what he saw. Early in their acquaintance, he had taught his employer some of the *ju-jitsu and karate* techniques—practically unknown outside his homeland at that period—which enabled him to render larger, heavier and stronger men helpless when the need arose. By making use of this knowledge, Ole Devil ought to be able to break the hold that was endangering him.

In spite of the torment being inflicted upon him, Ole Devil experienced neither despair nor panic. While he did not possess the extensive knowledge that Tommy would later give to his, as yet, unborn nephew—who would become legendary as the Rio Hondo gun wizard, Dusty Fog**—he had learned sufficient to be confi-

---

* *What the assignment was is told in:* OLE DEVIL AND THE CAPLOCKS.

† *Tommy gave the formula for making the stain to the Confederate States' Secret Service during the War Between The States, 1861-65. Belle Boyd, the Rebel Spy—who plays a prominent part in several of the author's Civil War and Floating Outfit stories—made use of it during her assignment told in:* THE BLOODY BORDER.

** *Details of Dusty Fog's career and abilities as a fighting man are given in the author's Civil War and Floating Outfit stories.*

dent that he could escape from the bear hug. There was one snag. His opponent might be a loud-mouthed trouble causer, but Ole Devil had no desire to inflict a serious injury on him as was possible when using Japanese techniques. So he was somewhat restricted in the methods he could apply.

As the man continued to exercise a savagely constricting pressure and grind him against the trunk of the white ash, Ole Devil came up with what he hoped might be the answer. One thing was in his favour. While his feet were still off the ground, his arms were free. Bringing them swiftly up, he thrust his thumbs into the soft flesh behind the angles of his assailant's jaw bone. It inflicted considerable pain but was far less dangerous than gouging the eyes or clapping the cupped palms on the ears. The former could all too easily result in blindness and the latter might burst the recipient's ear drums.

Gurgling incoherently as the agony bit into him, the man slackened his hold a little and, without meaning to, lowered his captive. He intended to twist and fling his tormentor from him. Before he could do so, Ole Devil delivered a stamp to the top of his left foot. Letting out a screech that was testimony to how little protection his moccasin offered against the impact of a solid leather heel on a Hessian boot, the man snatched his hands free and took what was meant to be a single pace to the rear.

Leaving the man's neck, Ole Devil's hands went to his chest and shoved hard. Coming while one foot was in the air, the push caused him to retreat farther than he had intended. Although he managed to avoid toppling over backwards, it proved to be anything but advantageous. Following him, the captain drove a left kick into the pit of his stomach and folded him over. Up flung Ole Devil's right knee, meeting the man's already bleeding nose and lifting him erect but helpless. Giving him no chance to recover, Ole Devil continued the attack. Shooting across his left fist with all the propulsive force of his slender, steel-wire-muscled frame behind it, he caught the side of the man's jaw. Spinning around, the burly trouble-causer landed face down and unconscious at the feet of the spectators.

Swaying a little, breathing heavily, oblivious of his bloody nose and torn shirt, Ole Devil swung his gaze so that it raked the crowd. Despite being dishevelled, his black hair still retained the points at the sides which he had cultivated. They gave his features an even more Satanic aspect and made him look meaner than all hell.

'All right!' the young captain gritted, bringing his scrutiny to bear on the small knot of men whom he believed had been behind the comments that had made him fight with the burly trouble-causer. 'If anybody else feels like taking it up, I'm willing to oblige him.'

The grimly delivered words brought silence to the onlookers, and the group at whom they had been directed refused to meet the challenge of the speaker's cold black eyes. After the speed and apparent ease with which Ole Devil had escaped from the bear hug, and the rendering of the man who had applied it *hors-de-combat*, none of his supporters were inclined to try and avenge him. Nor did they want it to be made too obvious that they were backing down. So they stood in uneasy silence, each hoping another would supply a way out of the dilemma. Those of the spectators who had favoured Ole Devil, tense and ready to back him if the need arose, were just as quiet. The remainder, who had merely come to watch and enjoy the fight with no great feelings either way, made just as little noise as they awaited developments.

'What's wrong, gentlemen?' demanded a deep and authoritative voice, before there was time for any other response to the young captain's challenge. 'Haven't you had enough fighting without needing to do it among yourselves?'

There was some restless shuffling of feet, but no replies, as the members of the crowd turned their eyes to the speaker. Looking as impressive as a bull buffalo among a herd of pronghorn antelope, he walked forward. Such of the spectators who were in his way moved hurriedly aside. While there were many who exchanged sheepish glances with one another, nobody seemed to want to meet his chilling gaze as it swept from face to face.

It was late afternoon on the 21st of April, 1836 and Major General Samuel Houston could claim to be one prophet who definitely was with honour in his own country. Events had proved that his tactics and assessment of the situation had been correct from the beginning.

Before noon on the previous day, the battle of San Jacinto had settled the future of the Republic of Texas in no uncertain manner. Helped by errors of judgment on the part of *Presidente* Antonio Lopez de Santa Anna, the courage and superior weapons of the vastly outnumbered Texians had won such a decisive victory that they had escaped the bonds of Mexican domination.* At a cost of only two dead and twenty-three lesser casualties, Houston's eight hundred men had killed six hundred and thirty of the enemy and taken seven hundred prisoners, including *el Presidente* himself, captured and identified by Ole Devil who had found him hiding and in disguise.

Despite the resounding success and complete vindication of Houston's strategy, there were still those who had no love for him. Seeking to detract from his now greatly enhanced status, some of them had seized upon

---

* *A more detailed account of the events leading up to and the battle itself are given in:* OLE DEVIL AND THE CAPLOCKS.

the one thing on which they felt he could be criticised. The result had been the fight which had just taken place in a clearing of the woodland that fringed the Army's camp at Buffalo Bayou.

'Anyway,' Houston continued. 'While you're here, others are benefitting by it. The post sutlers have combined to supply free drinks with which to toast our victory.'

Nothing else could have caused the crowd to disperse so quickly. The raisers of dissent had an excuse to retire without a loss of face. With them leaving, there was no reason for Ole Devil's friends to remain. The disaffected onlookers were drawn away by the lure of free drinks and the knowledge that the situation had no further opportunities for enjoyment. On Houston's orders three members of the unconscious man's outfit carried him away with them. In less than a minute, only one of the crowd was left with the General, other than Ole Devil, Mannen and Tommy. He was 'Deaf' Smith, Houston's oldest friend and very capable chief scout.

'Well, captain,' the General said, when the last of the onlookers were out of earshot. 'How did you get into the fight *this* time?'

'No excuse, sir,' Ole Devil replied, removing the handkerchief with which he had been staunching the blood from his nostrils.

'Well now,' Smith drawled. 'I wouldn't "zactly" say that. No sir, General Sam, I wouldn't at all.'

'Maybe you'd like to tell me, then,' Houston suggested, eyeing the leathery scout sardonically.

'Some of them North Texas bunch was blowing off their mouths 'bout you being too soft on the prisoners we took yesterday,' Smith explained. 'Then that big jasper got to saying's how we should give 'em a taste of what the boys at the Alamo and Fannin's crowd got. Was more'n a few starting to listen. So young Ole Devil ups and makes out he thinks the feller was blaming him for fetching Santa Anna in alive. Next thing, the two of 'em'd come out here to settle things perlite like and the rest'd forgot all about going after the prisoners.' He paused and a flinty grin came to his face. 'Reckon I'll sort of drift back for some of that free liquor now the fun's over. Tell you, though, I've a notion's anybody else who tries to make a fuss for the prisoners's going to be took sick real sudden.'

'Now what do you reckon "Deaf" could mean by that?' Mannen Blaze inquired sleepily and of nobody in particular, watching the scout amble away.

'I wouldn't want to *know*,' Houston declared drily, although he could have made an accurate guess.* 'How badly are you hurt, captain?'

'Not too bad, sir,' Ole Devil declared and he was not indulging in false modesty. 'A few bruises, none too serious, is all.'

'Do you feel up to taking a stroll with me?' the General wanted to know.

'Yes, sir,' Ole Devil assented. 'Let me have my gear, Cousin Mannen. I'll see you and Tommy back at the camp.'

'Yo!' Mannen answered in a lackadaisical manner, making what was already the accepted cavalryman's reply to a superior's order.

Accepting the bowie knife, Ole Devil slid its eleven inch long, two and a quarter inch wide and three-eights of an inch thick clip point* blade into its sheath. Then he

---

* At 'Deaf' Smith's instigation, the post sutlers kept an eye on the 'North Texas bunch' and slipped knockout drops into their drinks when they attempted to stir up bad feelings against General Houston.

* Clip point: one where the back of the blade curves to meet the main cutting edge in a concave arc. As in the case of the modern Randall Model 12 'Smithsonian' bowie knife, James Black made his blade with the arc of the 'false,' or 'top' cutting edge five and a quarter inches in length and as sharp as the main cutting surface.

thrust the barrel of the Manton pistol into the slanting, two inch broad leather loop attached to the right side of his belt, so that the butt was turned forward and could be grasped by either hand. Although the oblong leather pouch was on the back of the belt, it was not holding the three Browning Slide Repeating rifle magazines for which it had been designed. Instead of donning his hat, Ole Devil held it in his left hand and returned the handkerchief to his nose with the right.

'We'd better go to the stream along there and let you wash up,' Houston suggested as he and Ole Devil parted company with Mannen and Tommy. Walking in that direction, he went on, 'Do you know why I won't allow reprisals to be taken?—And I don't want any flattery.'

'You're not the kind of man who'd let that sort of thing happen, sir,' Ole Devil declared, meeting the General's gaze without flinching. 'Which isn't flattery, but a fact. On top of that, you know how some folks in the United States would react to any suggestion that you'd allowed unarmed prisoners to be killed.'

'That's about it,' Houston agreed, showing no surprise that the younger man had made the correct deduction. 'The only future for us lies in becoming a part of the United States, not in trying to exist as the Republic of Texas. There's a lot of opposition to it from the liberal-radical and anti-slavery factions. They make a lot of capital out of so many fugitives from justice coming here. To hear them talk, every settler in Texas is a blood-thirsty criminal. To have it said that we killed prisoners in revenge would give them proof of the kind of people they think we are. Treating the Mexicans we captured in a civilized and honourable manner will prevent them from having a justified grievance against us.

'Yes, sir,' Ole Devil agreed. 'Especially if our adherents point out what happened to our men who surrendered. But there'll be some in Texas, particularly those who

77

lost kin at the Alamo and Goliad, who won't take kindly to the idea.'

'Don't *I* know it?' Houston grunted, then his voice took on a gentler tone. 'But that's a cross I'll have to bear.'

As the two men reached the bank of the small stream, the conversation came to a halt. Nor was it resumed until Ole Devil had removed his shirt, washed his head and torso in the water and replaced the garment.

'I can stand off my critics by pointing out that the Alamo wasn't a massacre,' the General remarked, without showing any sign of resuming the interrupted stroll. Instead, he looked around for several seconds as if he wanted to make sure that nobody else could hear what was being said. 'Jim Bowie, "Buck" Travis, Davy Crockett and their men knew what they were letting themselves in for when they stayed on and they cost Santa Anna a whole heap more lives than they lost.'

'That doesn't apply to Fannin and his men, sir,' Ole Devil pointed out quietly.

'It doesn't,' Houston admitted bitterly, but in no louder tones. 'Fannin's indecision, stupidity, failure to obey orders, cowardice—put any name you want to it— was responsible for his men being taken. But people won't think of that, or of how he refused to try to reinforce the Alamo.* All they'll remember is how he and his men were murdered in cold blood and they'll want revenge.'

'In which case, it's lucky that Urrea wasn't with Santa Anna on the San Jacinto, sir,' Ole Devil commented, wondering where the conversation was leading. 'So you won't have to antagonize anybody by refusing to let them kill Urrea.'

---

* *A detailed examination of Fannin's failure to support the Alamo and of other events in Texas at that period is given in Walter Lord's* A TIME TO STAND.

'It's lucky in that respect,' Houston conceded.

'Why wasn't he here, sir?' Ole Devil asked. 'Our information was that Santa Anna had passed the word for all his troops to join him.'

'It seems that Urrea got word that the Yaqui had gone on the warpath in the south of Nuevo Leon and, seeing that a lot of his men came from that region, he took the Tamaulipa Brigade back to deal with them.'

'Which means he's over the *Rio Bravo** and well into Mexico by now,' Ole Devil drawled. 'Even if we had a force large and strong enough to send after him, doing so would ruin our chances of being accepted as part of the United States. The soft-shells† would say that letting us in would condone our invasion of a foreign country and bring international repercussions.'

'Sending a military force after him is the last thing I have in mind,' Houston declared. 'But, regardless of what he did to Fannin's command, right now Urrea's the biggest threat to the future of Texas.'

'How, sir?'

'Until Santa Anna took control, the Mexicans were too busy fighting amongst themselves to bother about what happened up here in Texas. After being licked this badly, it'll be a few years before Santa Anna'll get the restless elements tamed down and be strong enough to think of taking another stab at making us toe the line. But Urrea's a horse of a different colour. He's one general who hasn't been whipped and sent back home with his tail between his legs. That puts him in a mighty strong position for making a play at becoming the new *Presidente*.'

'Do you think he's got *that* in mind, sir?'

'*Santa Anna*'s sure he has,' Houston replied. 'I've had a couple of long talks with him. He's pot boiling mad.

---

* *Rio Bravo: the Mexicans' name for the Rio Grande.*

† *Soft-shell: a liberal-intellectual radical of the most pronounced kind.*

Lays all the blame for being licked yesterday on the Tamaulipa Brigade not having been here and claims that Urrea kept it away deliberately to make sure he'd lose.'

'That could be because he doesn't want to admit, even to himself, that he made a mistake chasing off after the Provisional Government instead of catching and dealing with the Army first,' Ole Devil suggested, mentioning one of the errors in Santa Anna's tactics which had helped to make the Texians' victory possible.

'There's more to it than that,' Houston contradicted. 'Santa Anna's no fool. He's had spies on Urrea's staff and they've told him enough to guess what he has in mind. He claims that Urrea wasn't acting on his orders to kill the prisoners, but did it to turn folks in the United States against him.'

'Do you believe *that*, sir?'

'It could be the truth. He's most likely heard of how high feelings are running over the Alamo up in the States. In which case, he'd not want to make things worse by having an even bigger massacre on his hands. Particularly one like that. It could stir up such a storm that Congress would have to take action.'

'And if that happened, Santa Anna would wind up fighting the United States,' Ole Devil supplemented, following the General's line of reasoning. 'No matter how it turned out, he'd be weakened and less able to keep a tight hold on things in Mexico. Anyway, sir, the trouble with Urrea ought to help us. It'll keep them occupied—.'

'Not for long enough,' Houston contradicted. 'With at least the "Landero" Line Infantry Battalion and the Tamaulipa Lancers out of his Brigade backing him, Urrea's got the best armed and equipped force in Mexico. Given that kind of support, he'll draw more in. Maybe not enough to take over straight away, but a whole lot sooner than anybody else, Santa Anna included, can do it. And, don't forget this, boy. Whoever gets in will *have* to come back up here and make another stab at whipping us. It's a matter of national pride. The main thing where we're concerned is, given time, we can become part of the United States. Without Urrea to take over and pull them together, we've won.'

'Somebody ought to do something about *that*, sir,' Ole Devil drawled.

'I can't send in an army——,' Houston began.

'That wasn't what I—or you—had in mind, sir,' Ole Devil stated, in a flat and emotionless voice.

'What do *I* have in mind?' Houston demanded, watching the younger man's Mephistophelian face with interest.

'Send in a few men and see if they could find some way to get Urrea,' Ole Devil answered. 'It *could* be done.'

'It could be certain death for whoever went,' Houston warned.

'Yes, sir,' Ole Devil agreed. 'But I've a few thoughts on how to handle it. Perhaps you can tell me if you think I'm right.'

'You've a pretty shrewd idea,' Houston conceded, after having heard the younger man's summation and conclusions. 'And I think it could work—But if it doesn't—.'

'I'm trying not to think too much about *that*, sir,' Ole Devil declared. 'And I'm going to do everything I can to make sure that it does work.'

Houston did not reply for several seconds. While he had sought out Ole Devil with the intention of obtaining just such a result, giving his approval did not come easily. The General had the greatest respect for the young captain and believed that he could become an influential force for the benefit of Texas in the future if he was given the opportunity. Sending him on the mission might, probably would, result in his death.

On the other hand, Houston had to balance the danger of losing a few lives against the possibility of gaining

81

a much needed breathing space. Time in which he could persuade the United States' Congress to accept Texas into its domain. At stake was the goal towards which he had worked for so long and for which many men had already given their lives. Despite his personal feelings, he knew there could only be one reply.

'All right, Captain Hardin,' the commanding general of the Republic of Texas's Army said, stiffening into a brace. 'Get Urreal'

CHAPTER SEVEN
Cut His Heart Out

CAUTIOUSLY riding his dun gelding along the bottom of a valley about five miles from the northern bank of the Rio Grande, in the middle of the afternoon of April the 24th, 1836, Lieutenant Arsenio Serrano of the Northern Coahuila Militia Regiment told himself that there were at least three grains of consolation to be extracted from his present situation. He was still alive, at liberty and, unlike the majority of the men who had marched with *Presidente* Antonio Lopez de Santa Anna from San Antonio de Bexar to the San Jacinto River, he was not returning home completely empty handed.

The only son of a wealthy *haciendero*, Serrano was in his mid-twenties, tall, slender and good looking. Few Militia officers had worn a formal uniform and he was no exception. He had on a high crowned, well made white *sombrero*, a brown waist-long, double-breasted shirt-jacket decorated with silver braiding and buttons, matching tight-legged, bell-bottomed trousers and high heeled black boots adorned with large-rowelled spurs. However, due to circumstances beyond his control, he was not wearing arms of any kind.

While there was a most efficient weapon in Serrano's saddlebags, he had no intention of advertising that he had it in his possession. From what he had seen during the period spent in hiding watching the battleground by the San Jacinto River, the Texians were not taking reprisals against the Mexican soldiers who fell into their hands. But they were unlikely to be so lenient if they discovered he was carrying *that* particular weapon. It was so distinctive that they were almost certain to recognize it and would know how he must have obtained it.

During the final assault on the Alamo Mission the men under Serrano's command had killed James Bowie. After his death, the young lieutenant had taken the famous Texian's knife as spoils of war. However, realizing that such a highly prized piece of loot would be claimed by one of his superiors—or even *el Presidente* himself—if they heard of it, Serrano had kept quiet about it. The other members of his detail had been killed in the fighting and nobody had learned of the part he had played in Bowie's death. To prevent the knife being seen and attracting unwanted attention, he had carried it in his saddlebag. That was how, although he had lost his own weapons, he still had it with him.

Serrano had taken no part in the battle which had ended Santa Anna's hopes of crushing the rebellion and had seen Texas established as an independent, self-governing Republic.* Intending to join a friend in another part of the camp on the morning of April the 20th, he had not bothered to don his sword and pistol. He had just mounted the horse which his orderly had saddled and brought for him when a wagon loaded with gun powder had exploded. High spirited at the best of times, the powerful dun had taken the bit between its

---

* Presidente *Santa Anna later signed the Treaty of Velasco, which admitted the independence of the Republic of Texas and agreed to its territorial boundaries.*

teeth and bolted. Although Serrano, excellent rider that he was, had managed to remain in the saddle more than a mile had fallen behind them before he could regain control of the frightened animal. By the time he had returned to the vicinity of the camp, the Texians' attack had been launched and the fighting was almost over.

Watching the battle from the concealment of some trees on a hill about half a mile away, Serrano had reluctantly concluded there was nothing he could do to help his companions. While he was no coward, neither was he a fool. He had realized that he would either be killed or taken prisoner if he went any closer. In the latter event, the discovery of the knife in his saddlebags might bring the wrath of the Texians upon him as it would be evidence of the part he had played in slaying Bowie. So he had remained in hiding for the rest of the day and had set off to return home after night had fallen.

Although Serrano had been eager to reach the *Rio Bravo* and gain the comparative safety of Mexican soil, prudence dictated that he took precautions. To reach the river had meant traversing the terrain through which Santa Anna's column had passed, looting, burning and pillaging as they went. The lieutenant's instincts warned him that it would be a most unhealthy region for a solitary and apparently unarmed member of the plundering army. So, to reduce the chances of being seen by other human beings, until that day he had travelled only during the hours of darkness.

His reasons for wishing to remain undetected were well founded but he was to fail in his aim of arriving unobserved at the Rio Grande.

Fired from among the post oak trees which coated the top of the valley's southern slope, a bullet ripped its way into the dun gelding's heart. Taken completely unaware, Serrano was just too slow in wrenching his feet from the stirrup irons as the stricken animal went down. Even as he heard the crack of the shot that had killed it, his left foot was caught beneath the collapsing horse. Although pinned to the ground, he was not otherwise hurt. As he placed his free foot against the seat of the saddle to try and liberate himself, he stared in the direction from which the sound had come. What he saw filled him with a sense of foreboding.

Led by a big, unshaven man wearing a wide brimmed, low crowned black hat, dirty black frock coat, very grubby collarless white shirt, Nankeen trousers and riding boots, four equally well armed, but no cleaner, riders were approaching in an almost leisurely fashion. Bringing their horses to a halt at the foot of the slope, they sat for several seconds studying the young Mexican. Their faces were completely devoid of pity or mercy, but he thought that there was something familiar about them.

'Why in hell didn't you shoot him instead of the son-of-a-bitching horse, Ernie?' the big man demanded, idly fingering the hilt of the huge sheathed knife that was on the right side of his belt and balanced the pistol that was on the left.

'Was figuring to, Dick,' answered the tall, gangling, buckskin clad rider to whom the words had been directed. He gestured with the rifle in his right hand. 'Only this fool hoss of mine moved just's I was squeezing off.'

'You're making a mistake!' Serrano warned, remembering where he had seen the men. Although he spoke little English, he knew enough to have been able to follow the gist of the brief conversation.* 'I'm a Mexican officer, not a *Chicano*.†

---

* As Serrano had no reason to speak English after leaving Texas, he had forgotten the little he had learned at the time of the events recorded in: THE QUEST FOR BOWIE's BLADE.

† Chicano: a Mexican settler in Texas, particularly one who supported the rebellion.

'That supposed to make some difference to us?' the big man inquired in Spanish.

'I've seen you in our camp more than once since we left San Antonio,' Serrano replied. 'We were told that you were fighting for us.'

Even as the lieutenant was speaking, he doubted whether the words would have any effect. There were white men who had supported Santa Anna out of loyalty to the Mexican citizenship which they had been granted on settling in Texas. However, for the most part such renegades were vicious and cold blooded opportunists whose sole motive was financial gain. Unless he was mistaken, these five riders belonged to the second category.

'That we are,' the big man admitted. '*El Presidente* pays us a bounty on every deserter we fetch in and you look like one to me.'

'Pays it dead or alive,' continued another member of the party. He was of medium height, with a narrow, vicious face and was attired in cheap town-dweller's clothing. Swinging from his saddle, he drew a long bladed knife from its sheath. 'So it's as easy to tote you back dead.'

He slouched menacingly in Serrano's direction. The rest of the men began to dismount and Serrano continued to push unavailingly against the saddle. He realized that telling them of Santa Anna's defeat would not save him. Once they heard of it, they would know there was nothing further to be gained by supporting the Mexicans. Nor could he do much in his own defense. They would not permit him to take Bowie's knife from the saddlebag, much less allow him to use it to protect himself.

'Cut his heart out, Wylie!' suggested a fourth man.

'Don't do that,' Ernie protested, leering evilly. 'You'll ruin them fancy duds he's wearing. Slit his throat from ear to ear.'

Strolling around the rump of the gelding, Wylie threw

a grin at his companions. It was a mistake. He should never have lifted his attention from what he regarded as a helpless victim.

Serrano had felt his temper rising as he watched the men and listened to their comments. From what little he could understand, he deduced that they were not interested in collecting a bounty for taking him back. Instead, they intended to murder him and appropriate his property. Ignoring the rest, he concentrated on Wylie. There was little enough the lieutenant could do, held down by the weight of his dead horse, but he had no intention of just waiting passively to be killed.

Without showing any indication of what he was about to do, Serrano twisted his torso towards Wylie. Shooting forward his hands, he caught the unsuspecting man's right foot as it advanced. Giving a sudden, powerful jerk combined with a twist and a push, he sent Wylie staggering.

'Get the bastard!' Dick commanded, lumbering forward.

While the rest of his companions began to run around the horse, Ernie leapt over it. Once in the air, he kept his feet together with the intention of landing on the recumbent Mexican's chest. Guessing what was planned, Serrano reacted with considerable speed and, in view of how he was situated, very effectively. Interlacing his fingers, he swung both arms around and up to the left. His linked hands caught Ernie's left leg at knee level and with sufficient force to deflect the descending feet. Letting out a startled and infuriated howl, Ernie felt himself being knocked off balance. Losing his grip on the rifle as he flailed the air in an attempt to regain his equilibrium, he finally landed on his back in a way which drove all the breath from his body.

Despite what Serrano had accomplished against his first two assailants, he accepted that he was merely making futile—if vaguely satisfying—gestures of defi-

87

ance. There was no way in which he could save himself from the rest of the renegades. Having separated, Dick and the other two were coming at him from each end of the horse. Although Dick was having to swerve around Wylie and Ernie, the pair at the other end had no such impediment. One was swinging up the rifle he held, meaning to strike their victim with its butt and his companion grasped a bell-mouthed blunderbuss with a similar intention.

At that moment, a wild, ringing yell reached Serrano's ears. It was followed by the rumble of rapidly approaching hooves. The blows were not struck. Instead, the two men joined their companions in staring northwards across the valley towards the source of the sounds. Startled exclamations burst from all of them but they did not display the kind of alarm which might have been forthcoming if the newcomers had been members of the Mexican army.

'Take it easy until we see if there's any more of 'em!' Dick commanded.

Although Serrano was grateful for the respite, he suspected that it would be brief and would do little to relieve his predicament. He had heard similar yells on the various occasions when Texian raiding parties were striking at Santa Anna's column during the pursuit from San Antonio de Bexar. However, even if they were some of Houston's men, they did not know that Serrano's assailants were renegades.

Turning his head and looking between the legs of the man with the blunderbuss, the lieutenant confirmed his suppositions regarding the possible identity of the new arrivals. They were three in number, riding side by side and none of them held a weapon.

Apart from a low crowned, wide brimmed black hat, the man in the centre wore clothing similar to Serrano's. However, his tanned face was that of an Anglo-Saxon and he had a pistol and knife on his waist belt. There was a rifle, its butt pointing to the rear, in some kind of leather container* on the left side of his magnificent dun stallion's double girthed, low horned saddle. To his left, the burlier Texian was armed in the same way and clad in the fashion of a working *vaquero*. Big and heavy he might be, but he sat his equally fine bloodbay stallion with the easy grace of a light rider. By far the smallest of the three, the last man was apparently an Indian of some kind. He had dark brown skin, with long black hair trailing from beneath the brim of a steeple-crowned black hat with an eagle's feather stuck in its band. A multi-coloured shirt hung outside a scarlet breechclout, encircled by a leather belt from which hung two unusual-looking swords. His legs were bare to knee length moccasins. He was as well mounted as his companions, on a powerful if fancy paint stallion, and rode just as capably. While the other two each carried a pistol and a sabre suspended from their saddlehorns, he had a quiver of arrows on his. An unstrung bow hung on two loops that were attached to the near side skirt of his saddle.

Almost as if they were connected by an invisible string, the three men came to a halt simultaneously and about twenty yards from where Serrano was lying. Making no attempt to take out their rifles, or the bow, they left the animals ground hitched by allowing the split-ended reins to dangle from the bits. None of them bothered to arm himself in any way. Instead, they advanced and adopted a shallow arrowhead formation with the slender man as its point. There was, Serrano decided, something compelling about him. Young he might be, but his attitude was that of a man used to commanding obedience.

'What's going on here?' the slender young Texian asked,

---

* *The use of a saddleboot for carrying a rifle had not yet come into general practise.*

coming to a halt with around seven yards separating him from Serrano's tormentors. His voice was that of a well educated Southron, but had a hard and unfriendly note.

'What's it look like?' Dick replied, sensing the other's disapproval and not caring for it. However, as he still did not know if the speaker had more men in the vicinity, he went on, 'We've just caught this greaser son-of-a-bitch and're going to kill him.'

'Why?' the sardonic-featured young Texian inquired.

Despite the lack of English, Serrano could just about follow the gist of the two men's words and he began to feel a trifle more hopeful. There was something about the slender spokesman for the trio which suggested he would not allow a cold-blooded murder to be committed.

'*Why?*' Dick repeated, raising his voice. 'We're going to pay him back for what them bastards did to our boys at Goliad and the Alamo. *That's* why!'

'Was he at the Alamo, or Goliad?' the young man wanted to know.

'How the hell do I know?' Dick demanded, glancing to where Wylie was rising and then at the other two men who were on their feet. Although Ernie had not recovered enough to help, they still had a slight advantage in numbers over the newcomers and were ready to back any play he made. 'He's a greaser and it don't make no never mind to me and my boys whether he was or not.'

'It does to *me*,' the dark faced Texian stated, showing no sign of being impressed or concerned by the quartet's menacing attitudes. 'Help him up and we'll ask him.'

For all his apparent calm, Ole Devil Hardin was alert and suspicious. He knew that he, Mannen Blaze and Tommy Okasi—suitably attired for their mission—were the first party to leave the camp on Buffalo Bayou since the battle. However, there were many Texians who had

90

not joined the main body of Houston's Army. In addition, Santa Anna had made use of bunches of renegades. Such traitors, operating for their own personal gain, could be expected to be roaming in search of plunder through an area that had been cleared when the Mexicans had advanced across it. He had no way of knowing to which category the five men belonged, so was disinclined to take chances.

'Help *him*—!' Dick spluttered.

'That's what I said,' Ole Devil confirmed.

'Just who the hell do you reckon you are?' Dick demanded, still uncertain as to how many more of the newcomers' party might be in the vicinity and hoping to find out.

'Hardin's the name,' was the reply. 'Captain Jackson Baines Hardin, of Company 'C', the Texas Light Cavalry.'

'*Hardin!*' Ernie yelped. 'Don't they call you "Ole Devil"?'

'I've been called that—and worse,' the young Texian admitted.

Ole Devil had decided to speak the truth so as to try and find out where the sympathies of the five men lay. If they should be loyal Texians, they might—probably would—be inclined to listen to reason. Since the commencement of hostilities, he had been growing in prominence. While he had not reached the heights of Houston, Bowie, Travis, or Davey Crockett, he was known to be regarded highly and had already built up a reputation of finishing anything he started. So, as he was clearly opposed to the quintet harming the Mexican, they might be willing to desist.

Throwing a quick look to the left and right, Dick noticed that his companions were showing less aggression than he had hoped to see. Even Cocky, standing next to him, was displaying a lack of resolution despite

91

holding a loaded and primed blunderbuś which would be a mighty effective weapon at such close quarters.

The big man was less easily cowed. Thinking fast, he came up with some pretty accurate conclusions. None of the trio wore what he knew to be the usual uniform of the Texas Light Cavalry. That implied they were on a scouting mission and not raiding with a Company. The presence of the strange looking 'Indian' gave strength to the supposition. In which case, it would be possible and safe to kill them. Not in the matter of duty, which had never concerned Dick, but because their horses and weapons were of good quality and would be worth taking after they were dead.

'If you're Hardin,' Dick growled, studying the newcomers' empty hands and speaking in order to gain time in which to decide upon a course of action. 'You've fought the greasers—.'

'More than once, *mister*,' Ole Devil put in, without offering to confirm or deny his identity. 'But I've never yet *murdered* one, nor stood by while somebody else did.'

'*Murdered*?' Dick spat back. 'What in hell did they do to our fellers at—.'

'I'm not going to argue with you,' Ole Devil warned, his almost gentle voice underlined with steel-hard determination. 'That man's a prisoner-of-war and General Houston says that all such are to be allowed to go home, not to be *murdered* in so-called revenge for the Alamo and Goliad.'

'So that's what Houston says, is it?' Dick sneered, drawing no special conclusions from the information.

'Those are the *General's* orders,' Ole Devil confirmed, laying emphasis on the use of Houston's rank. 'So you'd best do as I said and let this man go on his way.'

'All right,' Dick said, with what he hoped was a convincing air of resignation. 'If that's how *General* Houston wants it—.'

Allowing the sentence to trail off unfinished, the big man started to turn to his right. Then, moving with fair speed for one of his bulk, his left hand went out to grab the barrel of Cocky's blunderbus. With a quick jerk, he plucked it from its owner's grasp and, as he started to twist back to face Ole Devil, his right hand went across to begin shoving the hammer back to fully cocked.

Dick's actions had been carefully considered. Not only was the blunderbus more readily accessible than his pistol or knife, it was far more suitable for his purpose. At such close range, the spread of its charge could not miss the slender Texian and some of the balls might also strike at least one of his companions.

Providing, of course, that the weapon was discharged!

Clearly Ole Devil had some ideas of his own on the subject, as Dick discovered when the young Texian reappeared in his range of vision. Obviously he had not been taken in by the apparent submission to his demands.

Although Dick did not know it, the man with the rifle had given away his intentions. Knowing him, his companion had expected some kind of action and was starting to swing the weapon towards Mannen Blaze. So, as soon as the big man had snatched the blunderbus, Ole Devil and his cousin responded with a gun handling technique in which they had both acquired considerable proficiency.

With Mannen duplicating his moves at a slightly slower speed, Ole Devil's right hand turned palm outwards and closed around the butt of the Manton pistol. To slide the weapon from its belt loop, he used a system which would eventually be developed into the 'high cavalry twist' draw.* However, unlike the gun fighters who were to use it in the years following the War Between The States, his sequence of firing could not be

_____

* A detailed description of the 'high cavalry twist' draw is given in: SLIP GUN.

performed with a single hand. Instead, he used the heel of his left palm and not the right thumb to cock the hammer.

Before Dick's right hand could enfold the wrist of the blunderbus's butt or his forefinger coil across its trigger, Ole Devil's pistol had turned towards him. Fired at waist level and by instinctive alignment, the .54 calibre ball flew almost as accurately as if it had been aimed in the formal and accepted manner. Struck between the eyes, Dick went backward. He tripped over the dead horse and the blunderbus somersaulted from his grasp as he fell. Not a second later, his heart ripped open by Mannen's lead, the man with the rifle was following his companion down.

Whipping the longer *tachi* of his *daisho*—matched pair of swords—from the sheath on his belt's slings,† Tommy bounded forward as the shots roared out. Having expected trouble, Wylie was bending to retrieve his knife. In view of what had happened to his two companions and seeing the 'Indian' approaching armed with a long and clearly very sharp sword, he put all thoughts of fighting from his mind. Instead, he dived in the direction of his horse.

Neither Ernie nor Cocky showed any greater determination to stand their ground. The former had been rising during the conversation. While still not fully recovered from the effects of his landing on the ground, he was able to achieve a fair speed as he dashed towards their horses. Spinning around, Cocky bounded over Serrano's dead mount and joined the other two in fleeing.

'Let them go, Tommy!' Ole Devil called as the little Oriental went after the trio. 'Catch one of the horses if you can.'

---

† *The* daisho, *particularly the shorter* wakizashi, *was traditionally carried thrust through the warrior's girdle. Tommy Okasi had had his fitted with belt slings since arriving in the United States, as that made them more easy to carry when riding a horse.*

Such was the eagerness of the three men to depart that they ignored the mounts of their dead companions. Gathering up their reins, they swung on to the saddles and set their horses into motion. Although the other two animals were disturbed by the commotion, they did not attempt to bolt. Both moved off, but soon came to a halt because of their training to stand still when their reins were dangling free. Returning the thirty inch blade of his *tachi* to its sheath, Tommy had no difficulty in catching and leading the two horses back to where Ole Devil and Mannen were helping Serrano to free himself.

On being liberated, Serrano found that his leg was not injured in any way. He thanked and exchanged introductions with his rescuers. Once again, Ole Devil saw no reason to conceal his identity. He guessed that the young Mexican had escaped from the Battle of San Jacinto and had no connection with the Tamaulipa Brigade. However, to be on the safe side, he planned to give the other the impression that his party were engaged on a scouting mission in the direction of San Antonio de Bexar.

'I thought they might be,' Ole Devil admitted, when informed that Serrano's attackers had claimed to be renegades working for Santa Anna. He was relieved to know that the men who had been killed were not loyal, if misguided, Texians. 'The war's over, *senor. El Presidente's* in our hands, along with most of his generals. What do you intend to do now?'

'I was going home,' the lieutenant replied, impressed by the Texian's command of Spanish. 'But I'm in your hands.'

'Do I have your word that you'll go straight there and not take any further military action against the Republic of Texas?'

'You have it, *senor.*'

'Then you can take one of those horses and go. Aren't you armed?'

95

'I lost my weapons at San Jacinto,' Serrano confessed, but made no mention of Bowie's knife for the same reason that he had kept it hidden. 'It was my own fault—.'

'Help yourself to one of their pistols and anything else you might need,' Ole Devil offered, wanting to be on his way.

'*Gracias, senor*,' Serrano said and held out his right hand. 'Thank you, *Diablo Viejo*. I owe you my life.'

As the two young men shook hands, each knew that a debt had been incurred. If at any time in the future, Ole Devil chose to ask for something in return, he felt sure that Arsenio Serrano would give it without hesitation.*

CHAPTER EIGHT
Don't Make Me Kill You

ALTHOUGH business was far from flourishing since *Presidente* Antonio Lopez de Santa Anna had marched north to the Rio Bravo with his army, Luis Pandrosa—owner of the *Posada del Madonna*—was still critical of his only customers. They were not troublesome in any way, nor had they complained when asked to pay the somewhat higher than usual rate that he requested in advance. All of them gave the impression that they were used to being guests in inns as fine as any to be found outside Mexico City. For all that, and in spite of the prevailing conditions, they were not what he considered to be desirable company.

No matter how they were dressed, two of the guests were undoubtedly *gringos* and the third appeared to be some kind of an Indian. The slender man wearing

* *How Ole Devil requested repayment for the debt is told in:* THE QUEST FOR BOWIE'S BLADE.

the clothing of a *caballero* had produced a document on arrival which suggested that they had a right to be in Mexico, but Pandrosa had no way of knowing whether it was genuine or not. Being an efficient inn-keeper rather than a warrior, he decided to accept the trio at their face value, and just hoped they would leave in the morning as they had claimed was their intention.

'Our host's acting kind of edgy, and has been since we got here,' Mannen Blaze remarked languidly, after finishing a plate of the kind of *pastel de cabrito** upon which Pandrosa had founded a well deserved reputation among regular travellers along the trail between Monterrey and Matamoros. 'Could be that pass of our's isn't going to work.'

'I shouldn't think it's likely he's ever seen *el Presidente's* signature,' Ole Devil Hardin replied, leaning contentedly back in his chair. 'Anyway, it's not *him* that our pass will have to satisfy.'

Before setting off on their mission, the three young men had learned all they could about General José Urrea. Most of their information had been supplied by Santa Anna, who had proved most co-operative when informed by General Samuel Houston of what they hoped to achieve. Clearly he too appreciated the threat to himself and was willing to support any steps taken to remove it.

In addition to telling them a great deal about Urrea, including where he could most likely be found, *el Presidente* had supplied Ole Devil and Mannen with the type of passes that had been given to various important renegades as a means of identification and protection. Having already used such a document when going to

---

* Pastel de cabrito: *a pie made of small pieces cut from a kid too fat to be roasted, a little sweet oil and a sauce of chopped* perejil, *parsley, flavoured by eggs beaten in vinegar—or orange juice according to taste—being poured through the holes made in the crust to let the steam escape.*

collect the consignment of 'caplock'—percussion-fired—rifles which had done much to turn the tide of the Battle of San Jacinto in the otherwise outnumbered Texians' favour, Ole Devil was satisfied that the passes would be considered genuine.

The most debatable point, as the young Texian realized, was whether the documents would keep them alive long enough for him to be able to convince Urrea that he and his companions would be worth employing.

Parting company with Serrano, Ole Devil and his friends had continued their journey. Once south of the Rio Grande they had taken care to avoid coming into contact with the local population. They had a supply of food together with other supplies on a pack horse that had been left in hiding when they fought the renegades. Two days' travelling had seen them on the trail between Monterrey and Matamoros. So Ole Devil had decided that they would visit the *Posada del Madonna* in search of information. The *hacienda* owned by Urrea lay about twenty miles to the south-west of the inn and, if he was there, the owner ought to know. The young Texian had not yet broached the subject with Pandrosa, but he intended to do so before their morning departure.

Hooves drummed, leather creaked and wheels rumbled on the trail coming from the east. The three vengeance seekers turned their attention to the appropriate window of the diningroom. In a short time they saw riders and a coach coming to a halt outside. While they could make out only a few details, one thing was certain. The horsemen were wearing uniforms, which meant they were soldiers of some kind.

Soldiers so far south of the Rio Grande were certain to be members of the Mexican Army!

'Could be we'll find out how good the passes are real soon,' Ole Devil commented, watching Pandrosa throw a worried look in their direction before scuttling out of the diningroom.

A voice gave the order for the horses to be attended to. Soon after, footsteps sounded in the reception hall. In his haste, Pandrosa had not closed the door behind him and the trio at the table heard the same speaker demanding the two best rooms for the night. As they were occupying what Pandrosa had assured them were his finest quarters, Ole Devil and Mannen exhcanged glances. Although the inn-keeper's reply was too quiet for them to make out what he said, they guessed he was mentioning that point to the newcomer.

'*Gringos, here!*' barked the first speaker, showing none of his informant's care to avoid being overheard. 'What do they want?'

'They didn't tell me, *senor*, but—!' Pandrosa began, meaning to mention the documents which he had been shown by his Anglo-Saxon guests.

'Then, by the Holy Mother, they'll tell *me!*' the hard-voiced newcomer declared and the bombast in his tones suggested to Ole Devil that he was trying to impress somebody. His next words provided a clue as to who it might be. 'Don't worry, Bea—*Senora* Alvarez, I'll soon have it sorted out and settled.'

Without giving the person he had addressed an opportunity to reply, the speaker walked towards the dining-room door. He had the heavy step of one completely confident of his ability to handle whatever situation might arise. Or perhaps it was that he wanted to convince his audience of his ability.

The man who came through the door proved to be tall, swarthily handsome and clad in the uniform of a captain in the Tamaulipa Lancers. With his right hand resting on the hilt of his sabre, he swaggered forward exuding either real or assumed toughness and arrogance.

Lighter footsteps caused Ole Devil and his companions to look past the captain. A woman had followed him from the entrance hall and she now halted just inside the door. Despite the fact that she was clad in a broad

99

brimmed black hat and a matching two piece costume that was suitable for travelling but did little to flatter her figure, she gave the impression of being exceedingly curvaceous. About five foot eight inches in height, black haired, her stately beauty seemed to radiate a brilliance that would make most members of her sex feel inferior. Her langorous dark eyes went from Mannen to Tommy, then came to rest on Ole Devil. Returning her scrutiny, he could see how—despite her marital status—the Mexican officer might be eager to earn her approbation.

'What're you doing here, *gringos*?' Captain Escalier demanded as he came to a stop about six foot from the table.

'Waiting for coffee so that I can go to bed,' Ole Devil replied in an off-hand manner that implied he did not think his interrogator was of any great importance.

Sitting in a slumped manner, as if half asleep, although in actual fact tense and ready to take any action that might become necessary, Mannen waited to find out how Ole Devil wanted him to behave. He expected his cousin to produce Santa Anna's passes and introduce himself and his companions by the names on the documents. It might act as a means of establishing a more cordial relationship. So the events that followed came as something of a surprise.

'Get up and put your weapons on the table!' Escalier snapped, stiffening as if the slender young Texian had struck him across the face.

'Why?' Ole Devil wanted to know, refraining from looking at the woman although he sensed that his eyes were on him.

'Because I'm arresting you as spies!' Escalier explained, starting to tug on the hilt of his sabre. 'Get up, or——.'

Neither the movement nor the threat was completed. Rising, bending, and turning his right elbow outwards, Ole Devil gripped the butt of the Manton pistol. One of the advantages gained by wearing a handgun in that

100

fashion was that it could be drawn with considerable ease while sitting down. Twisting the weapon from the belt's loop, he swivelled its barrel to point across the table. As he did so, his left hand operated the hammer.

Much to his surprise, Escalier found himself staring into the muzzle of the pistol and its bore seemed much larger than the actual .54 of an inch. The clicking of the hammer being brought to fully cocked reached his ears. So swiftly had the move been made that his sabre was still no more than half way out of its sheath. Even if it had been drawn he realized that the speed with which the Texian had armed himself would have ruled out any chance of it being used.

'I don't think you are,' Ole Devil contradicted.

'I've a dozen men outside—!' Escalier started to warn, doubling the size of his escort instead of calling for them to come and help him as was his instinctive desire.

'And you've only *one* life, so you'd better let them stay there,' Ole Devil interrupted, making a point that the captain had already considered. 'They couldn't come and do anything quickly enough to stop me shooting you. Not that I'd want it to go *that* far—.'

'The devil—!' Escalier spluttered, almost beside himself with mortification at being placed in such a position with Beatriz Alvarez present.

'Don't make me kill you, captain!' Ole Devil requested, making a small yet very menacing gesture with his pistol as the Mexican officer's face grew angry indicating that he might be on the point of making some kind of aggressive action. 'General Urrea might not care for me doing that.'

'Would *that* bother you, *senor*?' asked the woman by the door.

'I've always found that it's a bad policy to antagonize a man who I hope will hire me, *senora*,' Ole Devil replied, glancing across the room. However, the pistol never wavered from its alignment and his gaze returned to Escalier before any advantage could be taken from the pause.

'In that case, *senor*,' the woman said, starting to walk forward. 'I don't think there's any further need for your pistol.'

'With all respect, gracious *senora*,' Ole Devil countered in a firmly polite tone, feeling confident that he had been correct in the way he had decided to handle the situation. 'I'd say *that* depends on how the captain feels about it.'

Hearing the name used by Escalier, the young Texian had remembered something that Santa Anna had told him. The presence of an officer belonging to the Tamaulipa Lancers enabled him to make a guess at the woman's identity. If he was correct, she must be Beatriz Alvarez. The wife of the Tamaulipa Brigade's Paymaster was, according to *el Presidente*, a person with considerable influence on Urrea. The captain's attitude, and the way in which she had acted when entering the room supplied Ole Devil with a clue on which he had based his behaviour.

As was her invariable habit when first coming into contact with men, Beatriz Alvarez had studied the trio at the table with a view of how useful they might be to her. She had dismissed Mannen and Tommy as underlings and so of no great consequence. However, Ole Devil struck her as being entirely a different proposition.

Due to having left his hat in the room he had rented, the young Texian was bare-headed. To prevent attracting attention which might suggest his true identity, he had shaved off his moustache and beard. He had also had his hair cut short, removing the horn effects which he had developed as a joke to emphasize the Mephistophelian appearance that went with his nickname. For all that, his face had a sardonic hardness which the woman found interesting. It suggested that he was a person worth cultivating. A trifle hot headed, perhaps, but capable of taking care of himself in a most effective way.

With the latter in mind, Beatriz decided to act as peace-maker. She had no wish to see Escalier killed because of his stupid pride and a desire to impress her. Not that she cared particularly about his death. She had already summed up his character and concluded that he would never amount to anything worthy of her attentions.

'I think you may have acted hastily, Alphonso,' the woman declared. 'It's not likely that these gentlemen would be sitting here so openly, knowing you had arrived, if they were spies.'

'Then why are they here?' Escalier asked sullenly, allowing his sabre's blade to sink back into its sheath.

'Perhaps you would care to explain, *senor*,' Beatriz suggested, when the young Texian did not offer to do so.

'Like I said, *senora*,' Ole Devil answered, returning the hammer to half cock and replacing the pistol in its belt-loop. He came to his feet, making it plain that he was addressing the woman. 'We're going to see General Urrea.'

'Why?' Beatriz challenged.

'I believe that he can use good fighting men,' Ole Devil explained. 'Would you care to sit down?'

'Well—,' Beatriz said, darting a look which showed that she did not care to accept while the other two were at the table.

'Go and take a drink or two, Otto,' Ole Devil commanded in English, then he nodded at Tommy. 'But make sure he doesn't get too many.'

'I'll see to it, sir! Mannen promised, lurching erect with an almost military precision. 'Come on, No-People.'

'Your *friends* are obedient,' Beatriz praised, taking one of the chairs after Mannen and Tommy had left.

'They're less friends than useful fighters,' Ole Devil corrected, guessing that the woman had understood what had been said between himself and his cousin. 'I've found that letting them think I accept them as equals keeps them loyal. Sit down, Captain.'

'I have to make sure that my men are taking care of everything,' Escalier said stiffly and without enthusiasm, having caught Beatriz's prohibitive head-shake. 'If you'll excuse me, *Senora* Alvarez.'

'Of course,' the woman confirmed.

'Tell the inn-keeper that the lady can have my room,' Ole Devil suggested. 'I'll move into——.'

'That won't be necessary, *senor*,' Beatriz put in. 'There's not so much difference in quality between any of Pandrosa's better rooms. Don't be long, Alphonso. I'll wait until you're ready to eat.'

'There's nothing like soothing a man's pride,' Ole Devil remarked when the Mexican officer was outside the room.

'I don't know what you mean, *senor*——?' Beatriz answered, but her tone showed that she did. She paused after *senor*, a note of interrogation in her voice.

'Von Richthofen,' Ole Devil supplied, that being the name on Santa Anna's pass. 'Count Franz von Richthofen.'

'You are German?' Beatriz inquired.

'Prussian!' Ole Devil corrected haughtily. 'Formerly of His Majesty's Hussars.'

'My apologies, Count,' Beatriz said with a smile. 'Why do you think that General Urrea would have need for your services?'

'Mainly because Santa Anna has no further use for them,' Ole Devil replied. He produced his pass. 'I've been working for him, but since the Battle of San Jacinto—of which I see that you've heard—I doubt if he'll be in a position to make it worth my while to continue. But General Urrea will.'

'How about your companions?' Beatriz asked. She ignored his comments on Urrea.

'Schmidt was my sergeant major in the Hussars.'

'And the Indian?'

'He's a Florida Seminole,' Ole Devil explained, watching for indication that the woman knew he was lying. 'For some reason, he fell foul of their main chief, Osceola, and had to flee for his life. He calls himself Tommy No-People because he can't go back. But don't let his size fool you, he's a very good fighting man with or without weapons.'

When selecting Tommy's identity, Ole Devil had decided upon the comparatively little known Seminoles of Florida. They had already inter-mingled sufficiently with escaped Negro slaves to account for Tommy's less Indian facial characteristics. Nothing the Texian could read on the woman's beautiful features suggested that she had knowledge of the Seminoles, or doubted what he had just told her. In fact, he felt sure that she had little or no interest in the Oriental apart from using him as a means of continuing the conversation without returning to the subject of why Ole Devil believed Urrea would have need of their services.

'You were at San Jacinto?' Beatriz asked, interested, having heard something of the battle from a Mexican soldier who had escaped on a horse and had reached Matamoros while she was there.

'No,' Ole Devil lied, but saw a way in which he could return to the reason for his being in Mexico. 'As soon as I saw that Santa Anna was falling into the trap that General Urrea had anticipated, I got well clear of him.'

'I don't follow you,' the woman declared and her whole attitude implied that she was genuinely puzzled.

'The General knew that *el Presidente* was doing the wrong thing by chasing after the Texians' Provisional Government instead of concentrating upon catching and defeating Houston's Army,' Ole Devil elaborated, wanting to impress Beatriz with his high—if possibly incorrect —opinion of Urrea's sagacity and tactical brilliance.

105

'And after Goliad, the Texians were going to be a whole lot harder to beat. So—.'

At that moment, Escalier returned. There was an air of secret triumph about him as he came to the table.

'I've told the men to get a meal in the barroom, Beatriz,' the captain announced. He sat down, carefully avoiding looking at Ole Devil.

'*Bueno*,' the woman replied, indicating the young Texian, 'You were wrong about this gentleman being a spy. He is Count Franz von—Ric——.'

'Richthofen,' Ole Devil supplied, concealing the thoughts he had regarding the Mexican officer's apparently innocent statement.

'Richthofen,' Beatriz repeated. 'And he has been fighting against the Texians.'

'Through loyalty to the Mexican citizenship that he had taken, of course,' Escalier sneered.

'Put any name you want to it, *hombre*,' Ole Devil answered in a coldly challenging voice. 'There are some in the Mexican Army who might call *your* presence here into question.'

'Why you—I' the captain spat out, beginning to shove back his chair.

There was more to Escalier's anger than the way the sardonic-faced *gringo* had used the derogatory '*hombre*' instead of his military rank. Not having been admitted into Urrea's confidence, his conscience was troubling him over his premature departure from Texas. While there had been some trouble from Yaquis, they were only a small band led by a renegade Mexican and they were neither sufficiently active nor dangerous to warrant the return of the whole Tamaulipa Brigade to deal with them. So he was worried by the thought that his fellow officers who had been captured with Santa Anna might regard his action as desertion. To have the point .mentioned by a man whom he already hated was almost more than he could bear.

'*Gentlemen!*' Beatriz snapped, half rising. 'Count von Richthofen! Captain Escalier! Must I remind you that *I* am here?'

The words had a cooling effect upon one of the men at the table.

'M—My apologies, Bea—*senora!*' Escalier gulped, remembering the way in which the *gringo* had produced his pistol and feeling not entirely ungrateful for the woman's intervention.

For his part, Ole Devil remained seated. Except for having started to lift and turn his right elbow, he did not appear to have moved. If Beatriz had been watching, she might have seen him tense slightly as he heard the second name she mentioned. Apart from that brief display of emotion, there was nothing to suggest that it held importance for him.

Lieutenant Paul Dimmock had had no premonition of what might lie ahead, but he had considered it his duty to learn all he could about his captors. So, in addition to identifying the infantry battalion that had carried out the ambush, he was able to supply Houston with the names and descriptions of the officers who had commanded the escort. From what Ole Devil had been told, he realized that he was in the presence of a man who, if not having actually planned it, had been a leading participant in the ambush.

'Count von Richthofen?' Beatriz said, turning her eyes to the Texian and looking at him in her most appealing fashion.

There were some people in Texas who regarded Ole Devil as a hot head who could not, or would not, avoid becoming involved in fights. They were wrong, for he was anything but that.

'Very well, gracious *senora*,' Ole Devil replied, and allowed his elbow to return to his side. However, his eyes stayed on Escalier's face and he went on, 'I was taking pay from Santa Anna for what I do best, fighting.

As he isn't in a position to continue paying me, I intend to offer my services to General Urrea.'

'Why would he have need of them?' the captain asked, in as tough a voice as he could manage.

Before Ole Devil could reply, there was an interruption. The thud of blows, intermingled with shouts of pain, rose from somewhere outside the diningroom. If the direction was any guide, they originated in the bar. Mannen and Tommy were there—as were the men who formed Escalier's escort.

CHAPTER NINE
Is This How You Fight For Mexico?

MANNEN BLAZE might look somnolent to the point of being dull witted, but he was far from that. Among other things, he was a pretty fair judge of human nature. So, although he did not give any sign of it, he sensed danger as soon as the six members of Captain Alphonso Escalier's escort entered the barroom. There was a burly, brutal featured sergeant and five equally hard looking Lancers. None of them appeared to be armed, but the Texian guessed that each had a knife concealed somewhere on his person.

Pausing just inside the door, the sergeant nodded to where Mannen—having crossed to ask where to find the back-house—was standing at the bar. As the non-com's companions began to walk forward, he caught one of them by the sleeve. While the rest approached the counter, he and the selected Lancer went towards the table at which Tommy was sitting.

Watching the four soldiers with the aid of the mirror behind the bar, Mannen might have thought that they

108

were coming merely to order drinks if it had not been for the other two separating from them. He noticed that the quartet were forming a rough half circle, heading straight in his direction. Knowing that Tommy could take care of himself no matter what might be planned—and feeling sure that more than a chance, innocent visit was taking place—Mannen continued to keep the four men under observation.

For his part, the little Oriental was equally as aware of the newcomers' suspicious behaviour. However, he gave no sign of it. Instead, he continued to sit and stare in front of him as impassively as if he had really been a Seminole warrior.

'Hey you, Indian!' the sergeant growled, coming to a stop at the table while his companion went around it to halt to the right and just behind Tommy. 'Get up and clear off, I want to sit here.'

Although Tommy spoke little Spanish, he had a pretty good idea of what the non-com had said. However, knowing that to obey would make no difference, he made no attempt to do so.

'You heard!' the Lancer barked, grabbing the little Oriental by the shirt collar with his left hand and clenching the right fist ready to strike as he dragged his victim from the chair. 'Get u——.'

The command was not finished, but it was obeyed; if not in the manner that its maker had intended.

Tommy responded with superb timing and the speed of a striking diamondback rattlesnake. Sending his chair skidding from beneath him, he came to his feet without needing to be pulled. Before the Mexican's blow could be delivered, Tommy snapped his right fist in a backhand swing that was powered by the momentum of his rising. The set of rock hard knuckles impacted against the centre of the Mexican's face. Blood flooded from his nostrils as he released his hold. Blundering backwards with his hands fluttering to the injured organ, he collided with a chair at an adjacent table. Sitting on it involuntarily, his weight caused it to collapse and he was deposited rump first on the floor.

'What the——?' the sergeant bellowed, starting to step forward.

Once again, Tommy brought a comment to an abrupt end. His left hand flashed out to hook under the top of the table an instant after the right had delivered its blow. With a surging heave, he flung it over so that the edge struck the non-com's forward shin. What had started as shouted words ended in a howl of pain. Instead of continuing to advance, he went backwards with greater speed than agility. Nor did his troubles end there.

Throwing a quick glance at the bar, Tommy went over the table as if he was playing leap-frog. On alighting, his small body sailed even higher into the air. At the pinnacle of his bound, the instep of his right foot curled out and made contact with the side of the sergeant's jaw. Already off balance, the force of the *tobi-mae-geri* 'jumping front' kick spun him around and sent him sprawling headlong across the room. Ramming skull first into the wall, he went down as limply as if he had been boned.

Hearing the commotion behind them, the remaining Lancers looked back. As was often the case when Occidentals came into contact with the highly effective martial arts of the Orient, they were amazed by what they saw. However, they were hard and tough veterans. So their shocked condition did not last for long.

'Get the Indian, Pedro!' shouted the biggest of the quartet, lunging towards Mannen who was still standing with his back to them. 'Come on, boys. We'll fix the *gringo*.'

Despite his apparent lack of comprehension of what was happening, the Texian had been watching everything. As he had expected, Tommy was fully justifying his confidence. However, that still left him with the problem of defending himself.

Although Mannen was armed, he made no attempt to draw either the pistol or the bowie knife. Instead, he twisted to meet his assailants with a speed that belied his normally lethargic movements. Having given his orders, the largest of the Mexicans was starting to carry them out. Unfortunately for him, his companions had not matched his rapidity of thought and action.

Gliding forward a step, Mannen swung his right arm. Before the soldier's hands could close upon the Texian, a massive fist connected with his *solar plexus*. He had never been kicked by a mule, but the sensation he experienced was very similar. All the breath was smashed from his lungs and, folding like a jack-knife, he went into a hurried retreat.

Having disposed of one attacker, Mannen gave his attention to the rest. Pedro had turned to carry out his companion's order, but the last two were moving in to attack. The man to the Texian's left was closer and faster, but the other struck him as posing the greater danger. While the nearer assailant was relying on bare hands, the second Lancer had reached for the hilt of the knife that was sheathed in the back of his tunic's collar. Before he could get the weapon into use, Mannen delivered a back-hand swing to his temple that knocked him staggering and caused it to fly from his fingers.

Even as the Texian struck the blow, he felt his left shoulder gripped and pulled. He was unable to prevent himself being turned, or to avoid the punch to the chest which sent him backwards into the bar. However, as his attacker moved in, his own fist shot forward. Connecting with the Mexican's face, the blow caused him to withdraw. The respite Mannen gained was of short duration. Starting to follow up his attack, two arms wrapped around him from behind and pinned his hands to his side. Making no attempt to retrieve his weapon, the

111

second Mexican had returned to the fray. Seeing the opportunity that was being presented to him, the first Lancer moved in with the intention of taking full advantage from it. As he advanced, he started to draw his knife.

Remembering that the small 'Indian' had in some way managed to fell two much larger assailants, Pedro was disinclined to rely upon his bare hands. So, as he went across the room, he slid a knife from its sheath in the top of his left boot. He considered that the weapon would give him all the edge he needed against the unarmed little man. Closing fast, with the blade of the knife extending ahead of his thumb and forefinger, Pedro made a stab aimed at the 'Indian's' stomach.

Although Tommy had left his *daicho* in the room which he would be sharing with Mannen, he was not greatly perturbed at confronting an armed assailant. Nor did he allow himself to become over confident. The Mexican handled his knife with sufficient ability to be dangerous even to a man highly skilled in *ju jitsu* and *karate*.

Facing Pedro as if offering his torso as a target, Tommy watched the knife as it was driven towards his mid-section. To the Mexican, it seemed that nothing could save the 'Indian'. Advancing his left leg, Tommy swung his other foot in a rearwards half circle which turned his body clear of Pedro's thrust. In addition to making the evasion, Tommy raised his hands almost to shoulder height. Holding them with the left thumb under the right palm and the fingers spread in a 'V', he sent them down to intercept, close on and jerk at his attacker's right wrist.

Such was the unexpected reversal of his fortunes that Pedro could not prevent himself being hauled forward, with the knife being directed towards the floor. He was even less able to avoid what came next. Setting his weight on his left foot, Tommy reversed the direction taken by his right leg. Bending its knee so that the thigh was parallel to the floor, he propelled the ball of his foot into Pedro's groin. Pure unadulterated agony caused the Mexican to release his knife.

Although the counter to Pedro's attack would have been sufficient to render him unlikely to want to resume it for some considerable time, Tommy had not finished with him. Seeing that Mannen was in difficulties, the little Oriental wanted to make sure that there would be no further intervention on his third attacker's part. Letting go of the wrist, Tommy folded his right thumb across his palm. Holding his fingers extended straight out, he chopped the edge of his hand against the back of Pedro's neck. Already swinging past, due to the impetus of his abortive assault with the knife, the Mexican went down like a rabbit that had had its back broken.

Like the soldier who was holding Mannen from behind, the man in front carried his knife at the back of his neck. Its blade was barely clear of the sheath as he approached, but he did not anticipate any trouble from the handicapped *gringo*. In that, he made a mistake.

Despite having his arms held so that they were inoperative, Mannen was far from helpless. Surging forward a couple of steps, against the ever increasing pressure exerted by his captor to prevent him from doing so, he swung his legs from the floor. With the knife coming over his head, the Lancer received both feet in the centre of his chest. Allowing his knees to flex, Mannen straightened them with a force that caused the man to almost fly backwards across the room. Chance rather than intent sent him in Tommy's direction.

Having just felled his third attacker with the *tegatana*, hand sword, chop, the little Oriental side-stepped to avoid being struck by Mannen's victim. Kicking his legs from under him as he went by, Tommy deposited

113

him supine, winded and stunned just beyond the other would-be knife wielder.

Some of the power Mannen had exerted was put upon the Lancer who was pinioning his arms. As he was already pulling rearwards, taken with the Texian's weight and violent actions, the soldier was thrown off balance. Nor did he have an opportunity to recover. Bringing down his feet, Mannen thrust himself backwards. By doing so, he drove his erstwhile captor against the firm and unyielding front of the counter. Crushed between the Texian's iron hard frame and the wood, the Lancer lost his hold. Turning, Mannen caught him by the front of the tunic and gave a swinging heave. Sent across the room, the man fell on to and smashed a table. Following it down, he made no attempt to rise after he landed.

Even as Mannen was dealing with the last of the escort, Ole Devil Hardin, Captain Escalier and Beatriz Alvarez came into the room. What they saw brought them all to a halt. Of the three, being aware of his cousin's and Tommy's abilities, Ole Devil was the least surprised. For all that, he realized that much of the ease with which his companions had defeated their attackers stemmed from over confidence on the Mexicans' part. A glance at the flabbergasted expression on Escalier's face told the young Texian that he had expected something *very* different. Ole Devil found Beatriz's reaction interesting. Anger rather than alarm showed on her face as she glared around.

'What caused this?' the woman demanded, turning her gaze to Escalier.

'Is *this* how you fight for Mexico?' the captain snarled at Ole Devil, hoping to lay the blame for the trouble on him.

'*You* know better than that,' the Texian countered, and looked at the woman. 'Ask my men, or the bartender, what happened, gracious *senora*.'

114

'It's obvious what happened!' Escalier protested, and his desire to gain exculpation led him to be foolishly indiscreet. 'They know about the money you collect——.'

'Keep quiet, you fool!' Beatriz almost shouted. Startled by the vehemence in her tone and the fury with which she had turned on him, the captain closed his mouth. Wanting to divert the "Count" from thinking about what had nearly been said, she went on in a milder voice, 'You behind the bar, what happened?'

'I—I—!' the man spluttered, being unsure of how he was expected to respond.

'You can speak the truth,' Beatriz stated. 'Who started the fight?'

Instead of replying, the bartender looked from the Mexican captain to the grim-faced young *gringos* and 'Indian'. All were watching him in a manner which was not conducive to peace of mind. While his instincts were to support his own people, he was all too aware that there was only the officer to stand by him if there was trouble. Yet his position would hardly be better if he told the truth.

'Well—I—that *is*—!' the man mumbled, trying to avoid meeting anybody's eyes.

'Tell the *senora* what happened, Otto,' Ole Devil commanded.

'They came in and attacked us, *senora*,' Mannen complied, snapping into a military brace and indicating the scattered, moaning, or motionless soldiers. 'Neither of us even spoke to them.'

'Very well,' Beatriz said quietly. 'It's obvious what happened.'

'Why'd your men do it, captain?' Ole Devil challenged, determined not to let the matter be glossed over.

'They've no love for *gringos*, or Indians,' Escalier answered, feeling decidedly uneasy over the way in which the woman's coldly accusing eyes were fixed on him. 'They always fight any that they——.'

115

'And yet, despite them being on a mission of importance, *you* sent them in here where they would find one of each,' Ole Devil said sardonically. 'That wasn't what I'd call smart.'

'Or me!' Beatriz agreed, her concern for possible danger overriding her usual tact and discretion. 'See to your men, Escalier. I wouldn't care to be in *your* shoes if they aren't able to do their duty in the morning.'

'May I join you while you eat supper, gracious *senora?*' Ole Devil inquired, conscious of the red flush that came to the captain's face as the woman spoke and turned away. Swinging around Old Devil moved to her side. 'Even if these men are unable to protect you, I and my men will offer to do so. From what I've seen of your escort, you—and the money you've collected for the General—will be safer with us than them.'

While speaking, the young Texian had been accompanying the woman from the barroom. Behind them, Escalier was glaring at their departing backs with ever growing fury. Finally it reached a pitch of homicidal rage that always lurked not too far below the surface of his nature. Snatching the sabre from its scabbard, he flung himself after the couple regardless of the possible consequences.

'I'll kill you!' Escalier screeched, swinging his weapon in a sweeping arc that had the side of the Texian's neck as its objective.

'Watch him, De——Count!' Mannen yelled, managing to avoid the error despite the urgency of the situation.

Even before either the threat or the warning reached him, Ole Devil was conscious of his peril. He had guessed, even hoped, that he might provoke some such response. Having heard the rasping of the sabre's blade leaving the scabbard, he was already looking back across his shoulder. Discovering how the attack was

116

being made, he set about countering it with lightning speed.

Starting to turn, and intending to yell for Escalier to stop, Beatriz felt a shove which sent her reeling clear of any possible danger. Before she could stop, or even turn her head to find out what was happening, it was all over.

While Ole Devil's left hand was thrusting the woman aside, his right flew across and enfolded the concave ivory handle of his bowie knife. Bending his knees and twisting around as he was drawing the weapon, he lowered his torso sufficiently to allow the sabre to pass over his head. Having taken that precaution, he turned his hand with the thumb downwards and lunged. Converging with the onrushing officer, who could do nothing to avoid his fate, the clip point passed between two of his left ribs and sank onwards until it found his heart.

Shoving himself to the right, Ole Devil snatched the blade free and allowed Escalier to go down. Nothing on the young Texian's face showed his grim satisfaction. One of the men responsible for the massacre at Goliad had paid the price.

Ole Devil doubted whether any of the others, particularly Urrea, would be so easy.

CHAPTER TEN
We'll All Be Killed

LOOKING at Beatriz Alvarez as he rode alongside her four-horse coach, Ole Devil Hardin wondered if he might have committed a serious error of judgement the previous night. Until he had discovered Captain Alphonso Escalier's identity (one of the killers at the Goliad massacre) he had been content to act out the part

117

of a character who was willing to let the woman act as peace-maker. However, on learning that Escalier was one of the officers actively involved in the massacre of Fannin's command at Goliad, he had behaved in such a way that an attack was provoked thereby allowing him to take the appropriate action in return.

Nothing Beatriz had said or done after the killing suggested her feelings went beyond concern for the safety of the money which she had collected and was delivering to General José Urrea. While she had been impressed by Ole Devil's astute deduction, she had neither confirmed nor denied that the money had been donated for the purpose of overthrowing *Presidente* Antonio Lopez de Santa Anna. The young Texian had been too wise to press the matter in the face of her obvious reluctance to discuss it. Instead, he had repeated his offer to accompany her and had assured her that he would be able to overcome any objections to his presence raised by the members of her original escort. Apparently satisfied that he could be trusted, she had accepted and asked him to be her guest while she ate.

During the meal and until retiring for the night, Beatriz had proved attentive. She had shown a friendly interest in Ole Devil, which had seemed to hold a possibility of developing into a much more intimate acquaintance in the near future if he played his cards right. It was, he conceded, very well done, and he felt sure that more than one man had fallen for similar treatment.

For his part, the young Texian had stuck to the story line that he had arranged with his companions. They had discussed it in order to ensure that there would be no major discrepancies if they should be questioned at a later date. He had left the woman with the impression that he was a former officer in the Prussian Army whose ambitions had caused him to leave his homeland under a cloud. Questioned about his presence in Texas, he had

118

explained that he was there trying to make his fortune, and had been serving Santa Anna as a combined spy and raider. By the time he was through describing some of his 'activities', he felt sure that she regarded him as being tough, ruthless and not over-burdened with scruples. The type of adventurer, in fact, who would be willing to take part in any kind of dangerous endeavour— even if it would mean turning against a former employer —provided that it was profitable.

The promises he had made to Beatriz regarding her escort did not prove too difficult for him to keep. Although he had doubted whether the soldiers would be in any condition to resume hostilities, he still took the precaution of making sure they did not come into contact with Mannen Blaze and Tommy Okasi. When the sergeant was conscious enough to understand what was said, Beatriz and Ole Devil told him of Escalier's death. As the captain had not been the type of officer to inspire loyalty or respect, the news had had little effect. Moreover, the non-com had heard enough to gather that the woman was not pleased about the fight between the escort and their opponents. Knowing the kind of influence she wielded, he decided it would be advisable not to attempt reprisals.

That morning, before moving off, Beatriz had informed the escort that Ole Devil's party would be travelling with them. Despite their antipathy towards *gringos* and Indians, the six soldiers had not raised any strenuous objections to the young Texian assuming command. In addition to the woman having stated that she was in agreement with the idea, they had all been in the army for long enough to recognize a real tough leader when confronted by one. There was a brief spell of sullenness, but after Ole Devil had turned the full force of his personality upon them, Beatriz noticed that they were soon moving with an alacrity that was usually accorded only to Major Carlos Badillo.

119

For all that Ole Devil had apparently earned the woman's approbation, he could not help speculating on how the news of Escalier's death would be received by Urrea and the other officers.

The young Texian's thoughts on the subject were brought to an abrupt end. They were about eight miles beyond the *Posada del Madonna*, on the trail leading to Urrea's *hacienda*. Riding at the head of the column, Sergeant Moreno let out a yell and pointed to the left. Looking in that direction, Ole Devil had no difficulty in locating the cause of the non-com's actions.

A number of horsemen were coming into view over a ridge about half a mile away. There appeared to be around two dozen of them. All but one were bareheaded, with shoulder long black hair. The exception had on the attire of a *vaquero* and appeared to be the only Mexican present. Of the remainder, some wore no more than breech-clouts and moccasins. Others had on either buckskin vests or odd items—such as jackets, shirts or trousers—of more civilized origin. All, including the exception, were well armed. Their weapons were a mixture of rifles, lances, or bows and arrows.

'It's the Yaquis!' Moreno bellowed, setting his spurs to the flanks of his horse. 'Whip up the team, driver!'

'Don't do that!' Ole Devil contradicted in a roar, sending his dun stallion bounding forward so that he could glare up at the soldier sitting on the coach's box. 'Stop the team, Man—Otto!'

Although the stress of the moment almost led the young Texian into an indiscretion, like his cousin the previous evening he managed to steer clear of a possibly dangerous error. His last words had been in English, but he suspected Beatriz had an extensive knowledge of that language and she might have noticed the use of the name 'Mannen' instead of 'Otto', remembering it at a later time if there should be questions raised regarding their true identities.

'Stop the team, driver!' Ole Devil supplemented in Spanish.

On the point of carrying out Moreno's order, the soldier was startled by the savage timbre of the young Texian's voice. Like his companions, he had been impressed by Ole Devil's aura of authority. So he ignored the sergeant and, even as Mannen came alongside the right hand lead horse, he began to apply the brake with his boot and haul back on the reins.

'What—?' Beatriz wailed, having watched the Yaquis in such concern that Ole Devil's words had not registered with her.

The alarmed squawk which burst from the woman was caused when she felt the coach brought to a halt instead of increasing its pace. While the deceleration was not excessively violent, it pitched her forward. Thrusting her hands ahead, she prevented herself from being thrown across the coach. Twisting around and flopping on the other seat, she stared out of the window. What she saw did nothing to make her less nervous.

At the command of the renegade who was leading them, the Yaquis sent their wiry little horses bounding forward. Waving their weapons and whooping war yells, they started to gallop towards the trail. Allowing them to go ahead of him, the Mexican followed at a slightly less reckless pace.

'Dismount, you men! 'Ole Devil yelled, reining his dun to a halt as soon as he saw the driver was obeying him. His words were directed at the Lancers. Springing from the saddle, he continued, 'Form a line on the side of the trail between the coach and the Yaquis.'

While he was speaking, the young Texian's right hand closed on the wrist of the Browning Slide Repeating rifle's butt and he began to draw it from the saddleboot. Showing an equal speed, Tommy quit his mount's back. The little Oriental led his horse forward and snatched the dun's reins from Ole Devil's hands. Taking both animals to the rear of the coach, he fastened them to the lashings of the boot. Then he pulled his bow from the loops on his saddle.

Guessing what his cousin had in mind, Mannen dismounted. Before he took out his rifle, he led his horse to the right side door of the coach and secured its reins around a lantern bracket. With that done, he wasted no time in extracting the Browning. Reaching behind his back to pull a magazine from his belt's pouch, he ran to where Ole Devil was standing.

Working with swift and unhurried speed, the slender young Texian was already preparing his weapon for use. Having no need to watch what he was doing, so skilled was he at loading the rifle, he was able to give most of his attention to the Lancers. Although Moreno had been ahead of the coach, the remainder of the escort were bringing up the rear. So, with the trail blocked by the vehicle, they were compelled to stop regardless of their inclinations.

'Dismount and form a line!' Ole Devil repeated in a commanding bellow, feeling the magazine stick as it reached the position from which its first loaded chamber was in alignment with the bore. '*Pronto!*'

It said much for the standard of discipline instilled by Badillo that the five Lancers responded as quickly as they did. They had learned that instant and rapid obedience to orders was less painful than acting in the tardy, unhurried manner which was the rule rather than the exception with the majority of Mexican soldiers. Without waiting to think, the men dismounted. Allowing their horses' one-piece reins to dangle, they ran to the left side of the trail. Holding their rifles, they formed a line between the coach and the rapidly approaching Yaquis.

The firearms had been one of the reasons why Ole Devil had decided to stand and fight. Taken from the men of Fannin's slaughtered command, they were of the

122

type already being called 'Mississippi', or 'Plains' rifles. Shorter and of heavier calibre than the kind known as 'Kentucky'* rifles, they had the advantage of being percussion fired and had been issued to the Tamaulipa Rifles as being more effective than their traditional weapons.†

From what Ole Devil could see, Beatriz had been correct when—making conversation at breakfast that morning—she had claimed the Lancers were well trained in the use of their new weapons. That showed in the way the soldiers brought the rifles to their shoulders, cocked the hammers, but held their fire.

Hardly able to believe his ears, Sergeant Moreno looked back as his horse was speeding along the trail. Discovering that the *gringo's* orders were being obeyed, he guided his mount around and headed towards the coach. Snatching the two pistols—also part of the loot taken from the Texians at Goliad—from the holsters on his saddlehorn, he almost threw himself from his horse and rushed towards Ole Devil.

'What're you doing?' the non-com bawled, realizing that the delay had ruined their already faint chances of out-running their attackers. 'We'll all be killed stop——.'

'Shut your mouth, you damned fool!' Ole Devil interrupted, glaring at him in a way that reminded Moreno of Major Badillo in a temper. It brought an immediate end to his protest. 'Guard *Senora* Alvarez, Tommy. Sergeant, come and take charge of your men. Don't let any of them open fire until there's no chance of them missing. All right, Otto, let's go.'

The young Texian's last five words had been in English, preventing the soldiers from understanding them. So there were a few startled exclamations as he and

* *The majority of 'Kentucky' rifles were, in fact, made in Pennsylvania.*

† *Badillo's troop had carried their lances during the ambush as being more suited to their task.*

Mannen started to walk towards the approaching horsemen.

Staring through the window of the coach, Beatriz was as puzzled as the soldiers by Ole Devil's behaviour. However, everything had happened so quickly that she still had not recovered her wits. Her first thoughts were alarming that the Texians might be collaborating with the renegades and had stopped the coach to make sure she fell into the Yaquis' hands. Before she could put this very perturbing notion into words, her doubts were resolved.

Studying the way their proposed victims were acting, the charging Yaquis were more delighted than perturbed. Even seeing the soldiers' rifles being trained on them did not cause them any undue alarm. They still had something over four hundred yards to cover and were, as yet, well out of range. Even when they came closer, the soldiers would only have time to fire one shot each. Nor would that be too dangerous. Past experience had taught the braves how to deal with such a situation. Seeing the puffs of smoke leaving the priming pans, they could slip over and hang alongside their mounts' flanks before the bullets were propelled from the barrels. Similar tactics had always worked in the past and they saw no reason why the present occasion should be any different.

'Stand still, all of you!' Ole Devil commanded, catching a movement out of the corner of his eye which suggested that at least one of the Lancers was starting to advance. 'Keep them back and under control, sergeant.'

'Do it, all of you!' Moreno snarled, his face showing puzzlement. 'Hold your fire until I give you the word.'

While the Yaquis were surprised to see the civilians coming towards them, they attached no special significance to the sight. Nor did they feel that there was any greatly increased danger as the pair started to bring up their rifles. Each brave paid extra attention only in the hope of discovering whether he was to be selected as a target, but none of them attempted to slow down.

Measuring the separating distance with his eyes, Ole Devil estimated it to be about three hundred yards. A long range, but adequate for his needs.

'Now!'

Hearing his cousin's word, Mannen stopped and settled the butt of the Browning more firmly against his shoulder. At his side, also having come to a halt, Ole Devil was taking just as careful an aim.

Two forefingers tightened on triggers!

When the rifles' charges detonated, the Yaqui braves received what was to be their first shock. The Brownings' mechanisms did not require an external priming pan, which meant there was no warning eruption of smoke. So both bullets were on their way before the Indians could think of taking the anticipated evasive action.

A horse, inadvertently hit by Mannen's lead, went down. Displaying great skill, its rider cut loose from its back as it fell and contrived to land on his feet without injury. One of his companions was less fortunate. Caught in the chest by the shot that Ole Devil had fired, the brave slid backwards from his saddle, dying.

Brave as they were, a sense of alarm swept through the rest of the attackers. Nor did what happened next dispel their fears. However, it was reduced slightly when the two Texians continued to hold the rifles to their shoulders.

Whatever thoughts the Yaquis might have regarding Ole Devil and Mannen's apparent madness in not doing anything they could recognize as starting to reload, none of them even came close to suspecting the truth. Few of them had ever seen even a double barrelled weapon, and the idea of one that could fire several shots in succession was beyond their comprehension, particularly when it could be done with the ease of the rifles in the two young Texians' hands.

'What are those *loco gringos* doing?' demanded one of the Lancers, having no greater appreciation than the Indians of the Brownings' capabilities.

'I'm damned if I know,' Sergeant Moreno admitted, scowling at the two Texians. 'Get ready to run for your horses after you've fi——.'

Oblivious of the advice that was being given to the escort, Ole Devil and Mannen were working their weapons' simple mechanisms. Neither looked at the other, but they had worked together so many times that the rifles spoke practically at the same instant.

The second pair of shots came completely unexpected to the Yaquis. This time, Mannen had held higher and his bullet tumbled a brave wearing a looted shirt from the back of a fast moving pony. Although Ole Devil's shot only wounded a man in the shoulder, the effect was satisfactory. Startled exclamations, which were duplicated by the equally amazed Lancers, burst from the remainder of the raiders. To add to their consternation, they saw that the Texians still did not offer to lower the rifles.

While putting the magazines through the reloading cycle, Ole Devil and Mannen selected their next objectives. Making sure of his aim, knowing that his life might depend upon it, the former killed a brave who was drawing back his bow ready to loose an arrow. Sighting with equal care, Mannen scored an impressive —if lucky—hit by knocking the flintlock musket which was being pointed at him out of its user's hands.

To have been fired upon twice was disturbing enough for the braves, but seeing the weapons discharged yet again increased their consternation. Brave as they undoubtedly were under normal circumstances, the unexplained always filled them with dread. Nothing they had ever come into contact with before helped them to understand how the two Texians could continue to shoot with firearms that ought to have been empty after a

126

single shot each. To the Yaquis' way of thinking, there could be only one explanation for the *gringos'* ability to keep on dealing out death.

'Spirit guns!' the warrior at the right end of the line screeched, putting his companions' thoughts into words and reining his horse aside as he decided that one of the magical weapons was being turned his way. 'They're magic! Flee before they kill us all!'

'Spirit guns!' echoed the other warriors. 'Flee before we're all killed!'

Even before Ole Devil or Mannen could squeeze off another round, the panic-stricken Yaquis were swinging their mounts away. One of them scooped up the brave whose horse had been shot, but such was the state of terror inspired by the weapons that Jonathan Browning's advanced mechanical skill and ability had produced, they fled without making any attempt to gather their dead.

Keeping the braves between himself and their intended victims, the renegade was following about thirty yards behind them. Although he saw what was happening, he was no better informed than the Indians and was equally perturbed at the way in which the rifles were working.

Even though he realized that the weapons' repeated fire must be frightening the superstitious warriors, the Mexican was taken unawares by the speed with which the attack was turned into a rout. Instead of having a line of men ahead of him, shielding him from reprisals, he suddenly found himself completely exposed. He snatched desperately at the reins, trying to follow the braves' example.

'Get that son-of-a-bitch!' Ole Devil snapped, lining his Browning.

The command was not necessary. Like his cousin, Mannen took no pleasure in what they had been doing. So he would have been equally willing to let the fleeing

Yaquis depart instead of trying to kill more of them before they were out of range. After receiving such a fright, they were unlikely to return and resume the attack. In fact, believing that their medicine had gone bad on them, they would in all probability call off their war trail and make for home as quickly as they could.

The Mexican was another matter. Leading the warriors against his own people, having them loot, burn, pillage and slaughter for his own profit, he deserved no mercy.

Aimed with deadly precision, the rifles cracked as the renegade's horse was broadside to them. Throwing up his arms as two lead balls tore into his vital organs, he toppled out of his saddle and landed across the body of one of the braves whom he had sent to his death.

Despite their belief that they had seen the last of the Yaquis, Ole Devil and Mannen continued to watch until they had disappeared over the horizon. From their rear came excited and puzzled chatter, suggesting that the soldiers were very impressed if unable to understand exactly how the attack had been broken and the braves driven off.

When the Texians turned and walked towards them, the sergeant and the Lancers stared as if mesmerised at the rifles. White-faced, showing that she too had no idea of what had happened, Beatriz was gazing from the window of the coach.

'How—How—?' Sergeant Moreno began.

'Our rifles are made so that they can fire more than one shot,' Ole Devil replied, indicating the magazine that he had removed. 'Have half of your men go to make sure that the renegade and the braves are dead. The rest can gather up your horses.'

'Yes, sir!' Moreno answered, showing admiration and none of the animosity with which he had earlier scowled at Mannen.

'I've never seen anything like it!' Beatriz declared as

128

the Texians crossed to the vehicle. 'When you made us stop, I didn't know what to think.'

'It was the only thing to do,' Ole Devil explained. 'There was no way the coach could have out run the Yaquis, so we had to make a stand. I was counting on our two rifles taking them by surprise. They'd never have seen anything like them.'

'I see,' the woman said quietly, looking from the Browning rifle to the young Texian's face. 'You're right about something else, Count von Richthofen. I'm sure that General Urrea can use your services.'

CHAPTER ELEVEN
I Didn't Think We'd Fool You

'IT'S clear to me that we owe you our thanks, Count von Richthofen,' General José Urrea declared, after Beatriz Alvarez had finished telling him of how the Yaquis had been driven off. 'You were right to make a stand instead of trying to run away.'

'It wasn't a decision that would have occured to everybody,' Colonel Sebastian Saucedo went on, throwing a meaning glance at Major Carlos Badillo.

Standing before the massive desk in the study at Urrea's *hacienda*, Ole Devil Hardin decided that the majority of the woman's audience were in favour of his tactics with the Yaquis. Even Badillo was not displaying any great feeling of grief on having learned that his second-in-command had been killed. That was probably due to the General's clearly expressed disapproval at Escalier's behaviour—as expressed by Beatriz—prior to his death.

There had been no sign of the Yaquis after Beatriz's

129

party had resumed their interrupted journey. Nor, apart from there being a much more friendly atmosphere between the members of the escort and Mannen Blaze and Tommy Okasi, had anything else of note taken place on their way to the *hacienda*. From the way the soldiers had behaved, it was clear that if not forgotten, the way they had been handled in the fight at the *Posada del Madonna* was forgiven.

On reaching their destination, the woman had invited Ole Devil and Mannen to accompany her to meet the General. Ole Devil had suggested that he would prefer to have Tommy along and she had agreed. Leaving their horses and bed rolls in the care of the escort, with Sergeant Moreno's promise that all would receive his personal attention and protection, the three young men had carried along their rifles and other weapons. Beatriz had said that Urrea would be most interested in the Brownings and Ole Devil, who was hoping to make use of them to strengthen his position with the general, had been pleased of the excuse to keep the weapons in his possession.

Obviously Saucedo and Badillo had known of the mission which had taken Beatriz to Matamoros. Both had arrived on the scene almost as soon as the coach had come to a halt in front of Urrea's mansion. Although the major had been puzzled by Escalier's absence, he had not mentioned it until the money was being transferred indoors from the coach. Nor had the woman enlightened him, beyond saying that the captain was dead, when he raised the question. She had promised that she would tell the full story in the General's presence, and the major had had to be content with that. Like the Colonel, he had studied the Texians and Tommy. However, neither officer had been willing to make the first inquiries. So the reason for the trio being there had gone unexplained until they were all assembled in the General's study.

While waiting outside the room until Beatriz had handed over the money and made her report to the General, her husband, Saucedo and Badillo, the little trio composed of Ole Devil, Mannen and Tommy had, compared notes on what they had observed since arriving at the *hacienda*. Urrea appeared to have allowed his *Activos* and Militia regiments to either disband or to return to the areas in which they had been recruited. However, the Tamaulipa Lancers and the 'Landero' Line Infantry Battalion were camped in semi-permanent lines just beyond the wall which surrounded the *hacienda*. That meant he had the nucleus of a well trained and armed fighting force readily available. In fact, after what had happened at San Jacinto, he had the strongest command in the Mexican Army.

Called in to be introduced and hear Beatriz tell of their meeting and what had followed it, Ole Devil had examined the men who were responsible for him being in Mexico. Working in order of their military seniority, he drew his conclusions about each of them.

Seen at close quarters, the young Texian did not form a favourable opinion of Urrea. While big, there was a dullness in his eyes and a complacent air that suggested a self indulgent nature. That he had courage and some military ability could not be doubted. He had won his rank during the struggle for independence from Spain and the bitter civil strife which had followed when it was attained. Yet he had nowhere near as commanding an appearance as General Samuel Houston, or for that matter the man he sought to depose, *Presidente* Antonio Lopez de Santa Anna. In fact, to Ole Devil's way of thinking, he did not have the aura of a natural leader.

Which raised the point of who was the power behind Urrea?

Whoever it was had, in all probability, master-minded the massacre of Colonel James W. Fannin and his command at Goliad.

131

Watching and listening to Saucedo, Ole Devil judged him to be a hard and tough man who had attained the rank of colonel by climbing on the bodies of his erstwhile superiors. To have done so suggested that he must have more than his share of drive and ambition. Uncouth, boorish, yet undoubtedly brave and with higher than average fighting ability both individually and as a leader, he appeared to have the drive to aspire to even higher positions. His qualities totalled up to form a powerful combination. Against them, his background and general outlook were almost sure to deprive him of the very important support he would need from the influential dignitaries of the Catholic Church and the monied classes.

Even if Saucedo was aware of his limitations, the young Texian wondered if he would be willing to act as the brains behind a more socially acceptable figurehead. Or if he would be subtle and tactful enough to prevent the man he selected from becoming aware of his manipulations.

As Ole Devil saw it, there was one major argument against Saucedo. Such a man, consumed with the intolerant and class-conscious bigotry of his kind, would never have permitted Badillo—who stood for everything he hated—to have achieved so exalted a standing in Urrea's eyes as to be allowed to attend a meeting of a confidential and possibly important nature.

Where the cavalry major was concerned, the young Texian had more than personal observation and deductions to work upon. On resuming the journey after the abortive Yaqui attack, he had ridden ahead of the coach with Sergeant Moreno on the pretext of helping to watch out for further ambushes. Fired by his newly established admiration, the non-com had been all too willing to talk. After satisfying his curiosity regarding the Browning rifle, the Texian had turned the conversation to the Tamaulipa Lancers. He had established that Badillo was an officer of some merit. He would have to be before he could earn the loyalty and admiration of a hard bitten veteran like Moreno. The sergeant had been voluble in his description of the feelings which existed between his superior and Colonel Saucedo. It clearly went beyond the traditional rivalry between a foot and a horse soldier.

From a personal observation of Badillo, Ole Devil concluded that he would be everything that was calculated to arouse the infantry colonel's ire. Of *Creole** blood, born into a wealthy and privileged strata of society far higher than Saucedo's humble origins, a product of the Mexican Army's Military Academy at Chapultepec, the major would not rest easily nor quietly in a subordinate capacity. That was proved by his presence in Urrea's office instead of his regiment's commanding officer.

Undoubtedly Badillo would not be beyond aspiring to the presidency of Mexico. He would also be realistic and intelligent enough to have decided that his *Creole* birth and comparative youth might be against him in attaining his desires. There were many in the country who would not approve of a man of pure Spanish origin becoming *Presidente*, and others would expect to be governed by a person of more mature years.

The question Ole Devil asked himself was would the major be content to play a waiting game and steer an older, more acceptable candidate into the position that he had set his heart upon attaining. While the Texian thought that he might, he would be unlikely to accept the continued existence of a dangerous rival like Saucedo. Of course, the opportunity to remove the colonel might not have presented itself.

Despite appearances, Ole Devil did not ignore Major

---

* *Creole: in this context, a Mexican of pure, upper class Spanish bloodline.*

133

Alvarez. On the face of it the Paymaster did not seem like a seeker after high office. Standing to the right of Urrea's chair, his whole attitude was that of a willing subordinate rather than one who hoped to improve his station. In fact, he put the young Texian in mind of something else. What it might be eluded Ole Devil for the moment.

There was one other possibility and the Texian did not overlook it.

From his first sight of Beatriz Alvarez, Ole Devil had felt that she was a woman of considerable personality and drive. Nor had later events caused him to revise his opinion. More than ever, she struck him as being ambitious, calculating and ruthless. However, she would know that no member of her sex could hope to become an accepted major factor in Mexico's destiny. So she might be accepting second best by steering a man into the position which she craved. Her husband would not do, so she might have settled for the General.

Like many before him, Ole Devil could not help wondering how Beatriz had become involved with such a man as her husband. It could, he decided, have been the result of a marriage arranged by their parents where the couple were not allowed any choice in the matter. Things of that kind happened, even in the United States, as Ole Devil had bitter reason to be aware. If he had guessed correctly, a woman of spirit would probably seek out some more promising material with which to achieve her desires.

'Was it necessary for you to kill Captain Escalier?' Alvarez inquired mildly, cutting into the Texian's train of thought.

'It was him or me,' Ole Devil replied, looking at Badillo. 'While I've no regrets, I apologize for having deprived your regiment of an officer, major.'

'With his temper, it was only a matter of time before somebody did,' Badillo answered. 'And you more than made up for it by saving *Senora* Alvarez from the Yaquis.'

'So you're a Prussian officer, huh?' Saucedo grunted, glaring in a hostile fashion.

'I am,' Ole Devil confirmed stiffly and shortly, with none of the politeness that he had employed while addressing the major.

'From what I've heard,' Saucedo growled, his antipathy towards the professional officer class being intensified by the ramrod straight figure before him, 'I'd have expected to see duelling scars on your face.'

'I've never met anybody good enough to put one on me,' Ole Devil countered, and was conscious of Badillo watching him with less antagonism.

'One thing puzzles the General,' Alvarez remarked, nodding to Mannen. 'My wife tells us that you are, or were, a sergeant major in the Prussian Army.'

'I was,' the burly Texian confirmed.

'Yet you can't be more than twenty-five years old,' Alvarez went on. 'You must have gained *very* rapid promotion.'

'I di—,' Mannen began.

'Don't bother lying, *amigo*,' Ole Devil advised and looked at Urrea in a way that seemed redolent of great admiration. '*Santa Anna* was taken in by my story about us having served in the Prussian Army, but I didn't think we'd fool *you*, General.'

'So you're not what you pretend to be?' Urrea asked, sounding a trifle puzzled but not entirely displeased by the slender Texian's obvious respect for his shrewd judgement.

'No, *senor*,' Ole Devil admitted. 'But I knew the real von Richthofen back home and believed he'd be more acceptable to Santa Anna than a couple of remittance men who've had to leave the United States—for their health.'

'So you're no more than fugitives from justice?' Saucedo sneered.

'Only because the three men we killed belonged to families with greater wealth and influence than our own,' Ole Devil explained, directing the words to Urrea and ignoring the colonel.

Watching and listening to the by-play, Mannen was impressed with the further evidence of his cousin's ability to take into consideration eventualities which might spoil a proposed line of action. Having envisaged that somebody might see through their deception, Ole Devil had arranged for a way to reply. If the hint of smug satisfaction on the General's face was anything to go by, he was far from displeased to discover that his visitors regarded him as being far more perceptive and intelligent than Santa Anna.

'*Senora* Alvarez tells me that you want to enlist in the Tamaulipa Brigade, Count—or whatever your name is,' Urrea said, throwing a scowl which silenced the comment Saucedo had intended to make.

'We do, *senor*,' Ole Devil confirmed. 'Our real names are Jack and Mylo Smithers.'

'What makes you think that the General needs to enlist more men, particularly foreigners?' Alvarez inquired.

'Good quality fighting men, which I think the *senora* will assure you we are, are always useful for what the General has in mind,' Ole Devil replied.

'And what do I have in mind?' Urrea challenged, after darting a glance at his Paymaster.

'That you'd make a better *Presidente* than Santa Anna,' Ole Devil answered.

'And why would the General think that?' Alvarez said mildly, when Urrea did not answer.

'Except for your part in it, over which Santa Anna had no control, he bungled the whole campaign against the Texians,' Ole Devil explained, directing his words to the General. 'He wasted hundreds of lives and almost

136

five weeks in taking the Alamo, then he celebrated a victory which had cost him more men than most defeats would have done. Even when he set out after Houston, having given him time to get well out of reach, he only started to hurry when following the wild goose chase of the Texian Government. The forced marches he made reduced his army to such a state of exhaustion that, when Houston trapped them against the San Jacinto River, they were easy meat. Against all that stupidity, you dealt with two forces, each superior in number to the defenders of the Alamo and received only a few casualties. A man of your tactical knowledge would never have made such blunders. In fact, you anticipated that Santa Anna was falling into a trap. That was why you turned back instead of joining him.'

While speaking, the young Texian wondered if he might be over-doing the praise. Urrea's face showed that the derogatory comments about *el Presidente* and the appreciation for his own ability were far from unwelcome. However, the General scowled at the reference to his withdrawal.

'Are you saying that we deserted our countrymen?' Saucedo snarled, also having noticed Urrea's change of attitude and hoping to capitalize on it.

'The General had only the interests of Mexico and the welfare of the Tamaulipa Brigade in mind when he turned back,' Ole Devil countered. 'He knew that Santa Anna was endangering the rest of the Mexican Army and that, in the event of a defeat, it would go worse for your men than those who had served under other generals.'

'Why should it?' Urrea asked.

'Santa Anna knew that the Texians might be willing to forgive him for what he had done at the Alamo, but they wouldn't over Goliad,' Ole Devil answered. 'So, as you learned, he made a point of saying that you had acted without his authority there. That the killing at

137

Goliad was on your orders. You knew that it would cost you the lives of every one of your men who fell into the Texians' hands. So, when it became obvious that Santa Anna was playing Houston's game, you wisely withdrew, not only protect your men, but to ensure that Mexico still had an army capable of defending its frontiers.'

As the explanation proceeded, it became obvious to Ole Devil that Urrea liked the theory which he was propounding. Either he had made a shrewd guess regarding the General's motives in not joining the main body of the Mexican Army, or Urrea was not averse to being supplied with a plausible reason for turning back.

'Do you know anything about the battle at San Jacinto?' Badillo inquired.

'I was too smart to let myself be trapped and wasn't there, but I stayed close enough to see what happened,' Ole Devil replied, and gave a brief, fairly accurate description of the fighting.

'How could so few Texians win so easily?' Saucedo protested.

'What happened to the prisoners they took?' Alvarez put in, before an answer could be made to the colonel's query. 'How many were executed?'

'None,' Ole Devil replied.

'*None?*' repeated three male voices, and all of the Mexican officers except the Paymaster looked a question at Beatriz.

'Not one,' Ole Devil insisted. 'There was heavy slaughter during the fighting. At least six hundred died and about twice as many were taken captive. But Houston would not allow any of them, including Santa Anna when he fell into their hands, to be executed.'

'I was told—!' Beatriz began.

'Whoever told you otherwise was either lying or mistaken, *senora*,' Ole Devil interrupted politely but firmly.

'How can *you* be so sure?' Saucedo challenged.

'I was in Houston's camp, dressed as a Texian, for a day after the battle,' Ole Devil replied. 'It was easy enough to do so in the confusion.'

'You went to a lot of risk and trouble—,' Saucedo growled.

'Incomplete information's no use and I always believe in coming prepared when I'm offering my services,' Ole Devil replied. 'I had an idea of the kind of things the General would want to know about, and I went where I could to get the answers. Like I said, it wasn't too hard, or dangerous, once the fighting was over.'

'That sounds reasonable to *me*,' Badillo declared. 'The Texians never had much idea of discipline.'

'Then how did they beat our army?' Saucedo challenged. 'Exhausted or not, Santa Anna had them outnumbered.'

'But they had better weapons,' Ole Devil pointed out. 'Their rifles matched against old muskets is what allowed less than two hundred of them to hold the Alamo Mission for thirteen days against the full strength of Santa Anna's army. And so many of them using caplock rifles, which would fire in the damp air of a cold and misty morning when flintlocks failed, caused the defeat at San Jacinto.'

'Did they have rifles such as you carry?' Alvarez wanted to know.

'Luckily for Santa Anna's force, they didn't,' Ole Devil answered, offering his Browning to Urrea. Then he took out and placed a magazine on the desk, continuing, 'If they had, many more Mexicans would have been killed.'

'Senora Alvarez told us about these,' the General stated, examining the rifle with considerable interest. How many shots will it fire?'

'I've only got five-shot slides,' Ole Devil replied, indicating the one on the desk. 'But they can be made to hold more.'

'I've heard about such things,' Saucedo sniffed, being

determined to discredit the young *gringo*. 'They're complicated, fragile, and misfire more often than they shoot.'

'Not this kind,' Ole Devil contradicted. 'It's so easy that even an enlisted man could be taught to use one. Neither Cousin Mylo nor I've ever had a misfire.'

'They certainly didn't today,' Beatriz supplemented.

'Do you know where to get more of them?' Urrea asked, showing greater animation than he had up to that point.

'Yes, sir,' Ole Devil confirmed. 'Santa Anna was interested and I put him in touch with the maker who lives not far from New Orleans. He had a hundred and was making more.'

'And if we give *you* the money, you'll go to fetch them for us,' Saucedo sneered.

'Not me!' Ole Devil stated emphatically. 'I know what will happen to me if I'm caught in the United States.'

'You say that Santa Anna was interested in them?' Urrea asked.

'He seemed to be *very* interested,' Ole Devil confirmed. 'An army, or even a regiment, armed with them would be a very potent force.'

'Huh!' Saucedo grunted. 'They'd just encourage the enlisted men to waste powder and shot.'

'From what I heard, that's the argument the United States' generals used for not adopting them,' Ole Devil answered. 'I can't see why it should happen if the men are trained and disciplined correctly.'

'I'd certainly like my regiment to be armed with them,' Badillo declared. 'If we can get enough of them, we'd be——.'

'There's one thing puzzles me about this *hombre*,' Saucedo interrupted. 'If he's been so close to Santa Anna, why haven't we heard about him?'

'There's a good reason why you shouldn't have,' Ole Devil replied, seeing a hint of suspicion come to the

General's face. 'He didn't just have me working against the Texians.'

'So you were spying on Santa Anna's officers,' Saucedo suggested, drawing the conclusion that Ole Devil had hoped he would.

'Them and the other renegades,' the young Texian conceded. 'There weren't many people *el Presidente* trusted——.'

'He seems to have trusted *you*,' the colonel growled, with the air of making a damaging point.

'No more than anybody else,' Ole Devil answered. 'But he paid me well and I gave him good value for his money. Only, as he isn't able to pay me any more, I'm looking for a new employer.'

For all his calm exterior, the young Texian was feeling anything but relaxed. All too well he appreciated the deadly dangerous game he was playing. His every instinct warned him that the next few seconds could make all the difference between life and death for his companions and himself.

CHAPTER TWELVE
We're Still Living On A Knife's Edge

NEVER had time seemed to pass so slowly for Ole Devil Hardin. From the start of the interview, he had been working towards this moment. If he was accepted, he could begin to carry out the far from easy task which had brought him into the centre of General José Urrea's domain.

At Ole Devil's side, Mannen Blaze lounged as if half asleep. Despite his lethargic attitude, the burly Texian was just as tense as his cousin. Although it took all of his self control, he contrived to avoid letting his true feelings show. So did Tommy Okasi. In that respect, the little Oriental was helped by the fact that he did not understand much of what had been said. However, sharing his companions' awareness of the precarious situation, he still maintained his usual inscrutability.

'I'll say one thing about you, young man,' Major Francisco Alvarez remarked. 'You've been very frank with us.'

'Why shouldn't I be?' Ole Devil asked. 'I want to make enough money to set myself up in a new life in Europe. I have come to a man who I feel sure can help me do it.'

'Some might think that would be a poor reason for hiring you,' the Paymaster pointed out.

'Others, with greater intelligence, wouldn't agree,' Ole Devil countered, looking straight at Urrea. 'They would know *exactly* how things stood with me.' His eyes flickered away from the General and returned as he continued, 'Which is more than can be said of others.'

'What does *that* mean?' demanded Colonel Sebastian Saucedo, having noticed that he was the recipient of a pointed glance from the young Texian.

'Only that, not being Mexican, I have no ambitions beyond doing my work so as to earn as much money as possible,' Ole Devil replied.

'I don't see what we would have to lose hiring him and his men,' Major Carlos Badillo declared, reaching the decision chiefly because he guessed his hated rival would be against it. 'From all we've heard they're good fighters, and we can always use men like that.'

'As long as we can trust them,' Saucedo supplemented.

'I'm willing to take a chance on *that*!' Badillo announced, glaring defiance at the colonel. 'In fact, if you don't object, General, I'll take them into my troop and let *Senor*—Smithers—replace Escalier.'

'Are you willing to assume full responsibility for them, major?' Alvarez inquired.

'I am,' Badillo stated. He had hesitated for just a moment until he saw the sneer on Saucedo's face.

'It's *your* decision, Carlos,' Urrea warned, having first glanced at the Paymaster and received what Ole Devil considered was a quick nod of confirmation. 'I put them in your charge.'

Noticing the rapid by-play, the young Texian suddenly realized what it was that Alvarez reminded him of. During Ole Devil's final year at school, one of the teachers had been paid by a wealthy parent to ensure that his son achieved a high scholastic record and passed a very important examination. Standing, apparently obsequious and unassuming by the General's side, the Paymaster looked much as the pedant had as he watched over and inconspicuously guided the far from bright student when others were asking questions.

If Ole Devil's impressions were correct, Alvarez must be the brains behind Urrea. What was more, the young Texian told himself, in all probability the Paymaster and not the General had decided to have the Texian prisoners at Goliad slaughtered.

'*Gracias*,' Badillo answered. 'I'll look after them. And I'd like to suggest that we find some way to buy enough of these rifles to equip my regiment.'

'Maybe Colonel Ortega won't agree to it,' Saucedo objected, although he knew that the titular commanding officer of the Tamaulipa Lancers had little actual say in the running of his regiment.

'I think he will,' Badillo replied, frowning at the reminder that he was—officially at least—subordinate to Ortega. 'He's not so old fashioned that he'll refuse to see the value of the rifles.'

'Why should your regiment get them, anyway?' Saucedo demanded truculently. 'You're supposed to be Lancers.'

'A lance is a poor weapon against a man with a firearm,' the major pointed out. 'And we may not find it so easy to take control——.'

'If we should agree to equip some of our men,' Alvarez put in, clearly not wanting any definite statement regarding their plans for the future to be made in the Texians' presence, 'how much would, say—three hundred—cost, Senor Smithers?'

'*Three* hundred?' Urrea almost yelped.

'Enough to equip *two* regiments, General,' Alvarez elaborated, laying an emphasis on the fourth word. Clearly the Paymaster intended to ensure that the balance of power between Saucedo and Badillo was maintained. 'What would they cost, *Senor* Smithers?'

'Ours were forty-five dollars each,' Ole Devil said, truthfully. 'But you'd maybe get three hundred at a lower price because of the quantity. He supplies the bullet moulds and powder flasks fitted with measures that ensure just the right amount of powder is fed into the chambers of the slide. You'll need percussion caps, plenty of them. Except for one thing, getting hold of all you'll need won't be too great a problem.'

'Go on,' Alvarez prompted and, to the young Texian's way of thinking, it was significant that he instead of the General had done so.

'According to the reports Santa Anna received, there was a lot of bad feeling against Mexico raised in the United States when word of the Alamo reached there,' Ole Devil obliged. 'He hadn't heard how the people felt regarding what happened at Goliad, but I'd be willing to bet it didn't make them any fonder of you—.'

'Carry on, please,' the Paymaster requested, when the comment came to an end.

'So the maker might not be too happy about letting it be known that he'd sold his rifles to somebody in Mexico,' Ole Devil continued. 'Which he'd almost certainly have to if he was paid in Mexican money.'

'But he'd sell them for United States dollars, if we had them,' Badillo guessed.

'He's a businessman, not a politician,' Ole Devil replied. 'So I reckon he would if the price was right.'

'We don't have any American money,' Saucedo pointed out. 'And the support *Senora* Alvarez raised in Matamoros wasn't anywhere near as high as—.'

'I can't answer for the exact state of our finances until I've had time to check on them,' the Paymaster interrupted and, despite his apologetic tone, it was plain that he felt the colonel's statement should not have been made.

'If we had enough would we be able to change it for United States currency?' Badillo asked and Urrea, to whom the question had been directed, threw his usual interrogatory glance at Alvarez.

'Arranging for an exchange shouldn't prove too difficult the Paymaster declared pedantically. 'It could be done through the bank in Matamoros.'

'We'd still have to organize the purchase and delivery,' Badillo said thoughtfully. 'Which means one of *us* will have to go to the United States and do it.'

'Who?' demanded Saucedo, his whole bearing redolent of suspicion.

'I don't think it's much use debating the matter further until we know whether we can raise the money to make the purchase,' Alvarez put in with gentle firmness. 'Also, my wife has been travelling all day. She is hungry and tired. So I'd like to suggest we leave things stand until we know more about it.'

'That's what we'll do,' the General stated, taking the hint, then his eyes went to the Paymaster. 'What about *Senor* Smithers and his men?'

'They'll have to be given accommodation,' Alvarez replied. 'And, as he is to serve with the Tamaulipa Lancers, he may as well meet the other officers. So I suggest that you invite him to join us at dinner this evening.'

'Of course,' Urrea agreed, with the air of having had

such an intention from the start. 'They're in your charge, Carlos. Take care of them.'

'*Si, senor*,' Badillo answered, but it was obvious that he did not care for the way the responsibility had been thrust upon him. 'I'll put him in Escalier's room, if that's all right with you?'

'It is,' Urrea confirmed, but not until after he had once more sought surreptitious advice from the Paymaster.

'Come with me, *Captain* Smithers,' Badillo ordered, darting a triumphant glance at Saucedo who was not troubling to try to hide his disapproval. 'I'll see to you.'

'*Gracias*, major. Excuse me, Senora Alvarez, General,' Ole Devil answered and went on in English, 'Let's go, men.'

'I don't like that damned *gringo*!' Saucedo announced in his usual hard and carrying tones, almost as soon as the door had closed behind them. 'Why didn't he tell you who he was in the first place, *senora*?'

'He had to use the name that was on Santa Anna's pass,' Beatriz replied, but her attitude implied that she did not care to be reminded of how she had been taken in by "Smither's" false identity.

'I suppose it's genuine?' the colonel asked, having no wish to antagonize the woman. 'The pass, I mean.'

'It's Santa Anna's signature,' Alvarez declared, waving a hand at the documents which his wife had brought in as proof of the two Texians' "identity". 'And I know that he did issue such things to renegade leaders.'

'I'm satisfied with him. I think he'll be useful to us,' Urrea put in firmly, speaking for once without first having sought guidance from his Paymaster. He still remembered the young Texian's admiration and complimentary comments regarding his brilliance. 'And there's certainly nothing he can do to harm us.'

'He might be a spy for Santa Anna,' Saucedo warned, never being willing to give up something that he had started.

146

'He *might*,' the General conceded, scowling unpleasantly at the continued protests. 'But *even* if he is, there's nothing he can do with el Presidente in the Texians' hands.'

'We've only his word for that,' Saucedo pointed out.

'May I make a suggestion?' Alvarez requested, and went on without waiting to be given permission. 'Even if he is working for Santa Anna, we can make use of him by giving him false information. In any case, it would be better for us if he is kept here. He's already seen and heard too much for us to let him go.'

'Why not shoot all three of them and make sure they can't do anything—?' Saucedo began.

'Because *I* don't want him shot!' Urrea barked, coming to his feet. Although he had no great objection to having executions carried out, he was determined to enforce his will. 'Is that clear, *colonel*?'

'It is,' Saucedo replied sullenly, stiffening into a brace. 'With the General's permission, I'll retire.'

Instead of escorting the two Texians and Tommy Okasi to their quarters, Badillo had stopped just outside the door as soon as the little Oriental had closed it behind them. Motioning for the others to remain, and looking around the entrance hall to make sure he was not observed, the major moved close enough to the door to be able to hear what was being said in the room they had just left.

'You've made a bad enemy in Saucedo,' Badillo warned, hurriedly ushering the other three across the hall, after having heard enough to suggest that the interview in the General's office would soon be over. 'He wants to have you all shot.'

'That doesn't surprise me,' Ole Devil admitted. 'Damned *peon* upstart. They're all the same when you give them a little authority.'

Satisfied that he had gained a useful ally in his feud with Saucedo, the major escorted Ole Devil and his companions up the main stairs. On the way, he gave them the gist of what he had overheard, with the exception of Alvarez's suggestion. He laid great stress on the fact that the majority of the objections had come from Saucedo.

'This will be your quarters, captain,' Badillo concluded, throwing open a door. 'I'll have Escalier's gear taken away.'

'This's really fine,' Ole Devil enthused, advancing and looking around the large and well appointed room. 'Far better than I've been used to recently.' He paused, then continued, 'It might be as well if I have my cousin and the "Indian" staying here with me. That way, Saucedo will have less chance of getting at any of us. You can say that it was your idea. That you think it will be easier that way to keep an eye on us.'

'That's a good idea,' the major praised. 'They can stay, if you don't mind having the "Indian" with you.'

'I've grown used to it, and he can be *very* useful to have around,' Ole Devil replied. 'They can eat in the kitchen, or have their meals fetched up here, whichever is most convenient for you.'

'I'll make arrangements for their food to be fetched up,' Badillo promised. 'And it will help if you all go out together. I'll have some of my troop close by when you do, just in case you should need help.'

'I'm obliged to you, major,' Ole Devil said, speaking with such sincerity that he might have been speaking the truth.

'If you're satisfied, I'll go and get ready for dinner,' Badillo answered. 'If you'll do the same, I'll come and collect you on my way down. My rooms are just across the hall. Until later, *senor.*'

'That's where he's gone,' Tommy stated, having opened the door for the major and closed it only far enough to allow him to make sure that Badillo had gone

148

across the hall. 'But I'll keep watching to make sure he stops there.'

'You don't reckon as how he'd've lied so he could sneak in next door and listen to us, do you?' Mannen inquired sleepily.

'Very old and wise Japanese saying——,' Tommy began.

'Which you've just made up,' the cousins chorussed.

'When you find an enemy has become your friend,' the little Oriental continued, clearly having grown used to such interruptions and making no attempt to contradict their justified claim regarding the age of the "saying", 'watch him very carefully to make sure that he is friendly.'

'Now that's real old and wise,' Mannen declared with lethargic solemnity. Then he became serious, although the change was only noticeable to men who knew him as well as his companions. 'It's all gone off pretty well so far, but I get the feeling we're a long ways from being out of the deep, dark and piney woods.'

'Keep thinking that way,' Ole Devil ordered. 'It's a good way to stay alive. We're still living on a knife's edge.'

'Should I slip, I'm going to make sure both feet go down the one side,' Mannen said quietly. 'Otherwise, it could ruin my chances of raising a family.'

'They're not what I'd call good right now,' Ole Devil pointed out.

'I wouldn't know about that,' Mannen protested. 'Why I've been told by more than one lil ole gal—.'

'Why sure,' Ole Devil interrupted, starting to unbutton his jacket. 'What do you make of them, Cousin Mannen?'

'There's a man coming from the officer's room!' Tommy warned before the burly Texian could reply. Closing the door, he went on, 'He's coming this way.'

Opening the door at the man's knock, Tommy allowed

him to enter. He had on the uniform trousers of a Tamaulipa Lancer, but his white shirt, sandal-covered feet and general appearance gave a clue to his status even before he introduced himself as Badillo's orderly, Tomas. Nothing the Texians or Tommy could detect from his behaviour and expression suggested that he might have noticed he had been seen coming from his superior's quarters.

'Major Badillo says that I'm to have hot water and anything else you might need sent up to you, *senor*,' the orderly announced, addressing Ole Devil. 'I will also arrange for your property and another bed to be brought in.'

'*Two* beds,' the slender Texian corrected.

'*Two, senor?*' Tomas asked.

'The "Indian" needs one,' Ole Devil pointed out.

'*Si, senor*,' the orderly grunted, but was too good a servant to show his real feelings on the matter of supplying an "Indian" with a bed. 'I'll arrange for it and for somebody to attend to you during your stay.'

'That won't be necessary, he does it,' Ole Devil answered, indicating Tommy with a jerk of his thumb. Then a harder, more commanding note came into his voice and he went on in English, 'Go and fetch the water.'

'S—!' Thomas, at whom the words had been directed, stopped, then said. I'm sorry, *senor* but I don't understand.'

'Show the "Indian" where to get my hot water,' Ole Devil repeated in Spanish. 'And hurry. I don't want to keep the major waiting.'

'*Si, senor*,' the orderly assented and looked at Tommy. 'Come with me.'

'He doesn't speak Spanish,' Ole Devil warned. 'But don't let anybody play tricks on him. Those two swords are very sharp and he doesn't hesitate to use them if he gets angry.'

'I'll remember and tell the other servants, *senor*,' Tomas promised, studying the little Oriental and edging by him as if afraid that he might explode. 'Ask him to come with me, please.'

'Know something, Cous—Count—,' Mannen began, after Tommy and the orderly were out of the room. 'What in hell do I call you now?'

'Cousin will do, so long as you don't take it any further, or at least make it "Cousin Jack",' Ole Devil replied. 'We can get away with "Count" by saying you got used to using it while we were with Santa Anna.'

'Likely,' Mannen drawled. 'Anyways, I think that Tomas *hombre* might have been lying when he said he couldn't speak English.'

'So do I,' Ole Devil admitted, tossing his jacket on to the bed and drawing the pistol from its belt loop. 'What do you reckon so far, Cousin *Mylo*?'

'That's one hell of a name you picked for me,' Mannen protested, then started to answer the question.

While waiting for the hot water to arrive, the cousins carried on a quietly spoken discussion. Ole Devil found, not unexpectedly, that Mannen's summation of the situation and general conclusions were much the same as his own. Nor was the similarity caused by a sycophantic desire to please a superior. The burly Texian was shrewd and a fair judge of human nature. What was more, having taken so little part in the conversation at Urrea's office, Mannen had been able to devote all his attention to studying the Mexicans' reactions to the various points as they were made. For the most part, Ole Devil had been compelled to concentrate upon the person he was addressing. So Mannen had formed a much better general impression of how the different aspects had been received.

'I got more than a tiny feeling that Saucedo and Badillo don't know about the money Fannin paid to Urrea as ransom for his men,' Mannen commented.

'I'll go along with you on that,' Ole Devil agreed. 'Alvarez didn't want too much talk about whether they could afford to buy the rifles or not. And it seems like they didn't get anywhere near as much support as they expected in Matamoros.'

The return of Tommy with hot water brought an end to the conversation. Nor, with a constant flow of servants fetching and removing property under the supervision of Badillo's orderly, did the cousins find an opportunity to resume it before Ole Devil was collected to go downstairs for dinner.

CHAPTER THIRTEEN
What The Hell Are You Doing Here?

WHILE Ole Devil Hardin and Mannen Blaze were holding their discussion, another conversation on practically the same subject was taking place in General José Urrea's *hacienda*. The two young Texians would have found it interesting, enlightening, and probably a little disturbing if they had been in a position to overhear what was being said, particularly with regard to themselves.

'That damned stupid, fat, useless fool!' Beatriz Alvarez spat out furiously, hurling her hat across the bedroom of the suite which she and her husband occupied. She had just dismissed her maid and his orderly, telling them not to return for an hour. 'It's no wonder that the people I consulted in Matamoros are so reluctant to support him. I doubt if I'd have collected as much money as I did if the news of Santa Anna's defeat hadn't arrived.'

'What was the reaction to it?' Major Francisco Alvarez inquired, but with none of his usual obsequious manner, as he began to unbutton his tunic.

'Just about the same as I told them downstairs when Urrea complained about how little money I'd brought back,' Beatriz replied, starting to undress with considerable haste. 'The few people who'd heard didn't seem prepared to believe it was true, and the *alcalde* did his best to keep them thinking that way.'

'That's to be expected,' the Paymaster said soothingly, knowing where the political sympathies of the mayor of Matamoros lay. 'He's Santa Anna's man and would want to do all he could do to prevent the news from spreading.'

'He did,' the woman confirmed. 'Santoval was there when he questioned the soldier. He said the *alcalde* warned him that he'd have him shot if he spoke of it after leaving his office. When we told the rest of our supporters about it, the general response was that they preferred to wait for more definite and reliable information.'

'I don't suppose we can blame them for being cautious,' Alvarez declared philosophically, dropping his tunic to the floor and peeling off his shirt. Although they were not bulky, there were hard and powerful muscles under his pallid skin. 'They'd wonder if it was possible that Santa Anna had guessed why the Tamaulipa Brigade had returned to Mexico and, by pretending to be defeated, was trying to trick them into showing where their sympathies lay. Don't forget, *querida*, we're dealing with businessmen, not idealistic dreamers, or liberals who pretend they're trying to make the world a better place for the poor people.'

'I've already found *that* out,' Beatriz declared bitterly, continuing to discard her garments with rapid and eager abandon. 'The Coun—"Smithers"—isn't the only one to suggest that what happened at Goliad will have an adverse effect on our future relationship with the United States. According to Santoval, the businessmen we were counting upon for financial support are afraid that public opinion in the United States will force Congress to ban all trade with Mexico if Urrea becomes *Presidente*. Damn it, 'Cisco, if it wasn't for that, with Santa Anna defeated——.'

'You did well to persuade them to part with as much money as they did, *querida*,' Alvarez stated, having no wish to continue discussing a subject which implied that he had made an error of judgement in suggesting to Urrea that the prisoners were massacred. He considered it advisable to ensure that his wife retained her respect for his omniscience.

'Getting it wasn't easy,' the woman admitted, showing relief and pleasure at the praise. She waved a hand to her luggage, which had been fetched up from the coach but was not yet unpacked. 'Our share of it is in my trunk. I'd liked to have kept more, but there wasn't that much——.'

'You made the right decision, as always, *querida*,' the Paymaster assured her, sitting on the edge of the bed. His eyes roamed over her gorgeous body, now clad only in a pair of flimsy white drawers. Raising his right leg, he went on, 'Pull off my boots for me.'

If any of the men with whom she had flirted in the interests of her husband's scheming had seen how swiftly and eagerly Beatriz started to carry out the menial task, they would have been amazed. It might have suggested to them that her apparently dull and uninteresting husband possessed unsuspected qualities that they themselves lacked.

Standing astride Alvarez's elevated leg, the woman grasped the heel of his boot in both hands. Helped by a shove from his other foot, she drew it off. Having repeated the process and set the boots aside with a greater care than she had shown to her own clothing, she flung herself on top of her husband as he sprawled supine on the bed.

'Mother of God! How I've missed you, Cisco!' Beatriz gasped, following an embrace which lasted for close to a

154

minute. They reversed their positions, so that her arms were round him and her naked and imposing bosom was ground into his chest. 'There's not another man in the world can come up to you—Not that any of them have ever——.'

'I don't doubt *that*, *querida*,' Alvarez said reassuringly as his wife's words trailed to an uneasy end.

'You can't imagine how it infuriates me when I see how people treat you,' Beatriz went on, nuzzling at her husband's face. Wanting to give further proof of her devotion, for she knew just how dangerous he could be when crossed or suspicious, she continued. 'Look at "Smithers" just now, giving Urrea credit for the things you had deduced and planned. It was *you* who realized how badly Santa Anna was conducting the campaign, possibly even leading the Army into a trap——.'

'What do you make of "Smithers", *querida*?' the Paymaster interrupted, drawing away slightly.

'Well—,' Beatriz began cautiously. 'I haven't had much time to get to know—.'

'You must have some ideas about him!' Alvarez growled, irritated by the evasive response. 'I've always valued your judgement. Is he what he claims to be?'

'He's been raised a gentleman, if his manners mean anything,' the woman decided, taking warning from the way her husband had spoken. 'Certainly his class is closer to Badillo's than Saucedo's. He's intelligent and, from the way he treated Escalier, arrogant and quick tempered. Such a man might easily have done something which would force him to flee to Texas. As *you're* satisfied that his pass is genuine, he must have worked for Santa Anna. *El Presidente* used renegades and "Smithers" would be clever enough to appeal to him as one who would be very useful.'

'Could he still be working for him?'

'You mean that he's been sent here to spy on us?'

'It's possible. We've known all along that *El Presi-*

dente would want to learn the real reason why we turned back.'

'Do you think that it's not true he was defeated at San Jacinto?' Beatriz asked, unbuttoning the front of her husband's trousers.

Instead of replying immediately, Alvarez rolled from his upper position and shoved the woman's hands away. Her question had started a train of thought and he wanted to consider it without distraction.

'He wouldn't take a chance on lying about something as important as that,' the Paymaster concluded, half to himself as he lay on his side ignoring Beatriz as she moved restlessly. 'Or if he had, he'd have told us that Santa Anna was either killed in the fighting, or held prisoner and awaiting execution.'

'Then he must have been speaking the truth,' the woman suggested, hoping to bring her husband back to a receptive frame of mind and give her the pleasure she was anticipating. She was completely sincere in her praise of his sexual prowess. 'Santa Anna might have intended to send him after defeating the Texians, and when the battle went the other way, the gringo could well have decided that he might as well turn what he had learned to his own advantage. Texas wouldn't be a very healthy place for a renegade and, as he told us, he daren't go back to the United States. So where else would be better for him than in the service of the man whom he guessed was planning to become the next *Presidente* of Mexico.'

"You could be correct, *querida*,' Alvarez said thoughtfully, for the summation almost duplicated his own. 'I think he deserves to be examined much more closely before we decide whether to have him accepted or rejected. Having seen the way he won Urrea and Badillo over, I agree with you about his intelligence. Handled correctly, he could be very useful to *us*. Apart from

156

anything else, I wouldn't be averse to having a man in Badillo's confidence.'

'Do you want me to sound him out and see what I can learn?' Beatriz inquired, knowing that her husband preferred to let her handle such matters so as to remain unsuspected in the background himself.

'It would be as well, *querida*,' Alvarez admitted, scooping her into his arms and assuming the upper position once more. 'If we find out he's not to be trusted, or won't be of any use to us, we can always have Urrea get rid of him.'

Having other things on her mind, Beatriz did not reply.

* * * * *

Ole Devil Hardin found it somewhat disconcerting to accompany Major Carlos Badillo into the *hacienda*'s big and well lit diningroom. As he entered he realised he was the target of everybody's eyes. Apart from the people he had met in Urrea's office, there were half a dozen officers from each of the two regiments, a couple of priests and ten women. In addition to having washed and shaved, Tommy Okasi had done a good job of tidying the young Texian's clothing and had put a high polish to his boots. Although he had left the Manton pistol in his quarters, the bowie knife hung sheathed on his belt. Badillo had raised no objection to the weapon on collecting him and had, in fact, given permission for him to retain it on his person.

Looking around, the young Texian deduced that the various officers were aware of their respective superiors' antipathy towards one another and, in part at least, shared it. That was, he decided as he studied the two groups, not entirely unexpected. To a man, the members of the Tamaulipa Lancers originated from the land-owning, *caballero* class. On the other hand, the officers of the 'Landero' Line Infantry Battalion were just as obviously from a lower level of society and clearly ill at

157

east in such comparatively opulent surroundings. Despite the fact that most of the females present were with the horse soldiers, the infantrymen made no attempt to mingle.

If the scowls being thrown Ole Devil's way from the infantry party meant anything, either Colonel Sebastian Saucedo had made known his sentiments or his men hated all *gringos* indiscriminately. However, seeing the General nodding amiably to the young Texian, they contented themselves with frowns and made no attempt to approach him.

On the other hand, perhaps because of their rivals' attitudes, the Lancers behaved in a cordial fashion when Badillo took Ole Devil across and introduced him. If any of them felt resentment, or hostility, over what had happened to Captain Escalier, they took care to conceal their emotions. The Texian deduced that they might have some reservations about granting him complete acceptance, but were willing to be sociable because that was what the major wanted.

Before there could be any extensive conversation, Urrea asked his guests to take their seats. Ole Devil was not greatly surprised when the Lancer officers went to one side of the table and the infantrymen to the other. For his part, the young Texian was seated near the head of the table between Badillo and one of the female guests. Assuming that she was the partner of the officer on her other side, Ole Devil was careful not to do anything which might provoke resentment. During the time he had spent in Texas, he had dined sufficiently often with well-to-do *Chicano* families to have learned the acceptable social graces. Conscious of Badillo's subordinates watching surreptitiously, he felt sure that he was conveying the correct impression. They would be more willing to stand by him against the uncouth foot soldiers if they believed he came from a background similar to their own. Before the main course was served, they appeared to be satisfied on that point.

Sitting at the bottom of the table, facing Urrea along its length, Beatriz Alvarez studied Ole Devil. So far she had made no attempt to begin her proposed investigations. She had no wish to arouse the jealousies of the General, Saucedo or Badillo; each of whom had cause to believe she preferred him far more than her husband. During their brief contact before the meal, she had treated the young Texian politely yet with a hint of condescension, her attitude implying that, while she was grateful to him, he was after all merely a social inferior who had done no more than his duty by rescuing her. Such behaviour, she had felt sure, would make him more amenable to cultivation when a suitable opportunity arose.

Although the woman had hoped to make the preliminary steps in her investigation later in the evening, the chance to do so was denied her. While the servants were passing around cups of coffee, Urrea's *major domo* entered, followed by an exhausted-looking man in a trail dirty, dishevelled military uniform. Ole Devil identified the newcomer's attire as that of a captain in a cavalry regiment under the command of General Martin Perfecto Cós. Obviously he had escaped either during or since the battle, but that did not explain why he had come—clearly at considerable speed—to Urrea's headquarters. One thing was for sure, the General, among others, recognized the man.

'Captain Seguin!' Urrea boomed, lurching hurriedly to his feet and tossing aside his napkin. 'Where did you come fr—?'

'General!' the newcomer interrupted, advancing hurriedly. 'I've got some ba—important news for you.'

'What is it?' Urrea demanded.

'It's important,' Seguin repeated and threw a pointed

look at the other officers who were making their interest obvious. 'And confidential.'

'Perhaps we had better hear it in your office, General,' Alvarez suggested from his place at Saucedo's right.

'That would be best,' the colonel agreed, also rising and his whole attitude showed that he intended to be present during the interview.

Watching Badillo stand, obviously equally determined to attend the meeting, Ole Devil thought fast. He had an unpleasant suspicion of what had brought Seguin to Urrea's *hacienda* and he did not care for some of the possibilities that might occur. So he decided that it would be advisable for him to hear the news which the captain had ridden so far and so hard to deliver. That raised the problem of how to satisfy his curiosity. Attempting to duplicate Badillo's eavesdropping at the door would be impossible in the face of the considerable coming and going in the main hall. Nor would the chances be better outside the building. Not only was there nowhere to hide near the office's window, but the area was patrolled regularly by sentries who knew better than to shirk their duties.

There was, Ole Devil concluded, only one way in which he might achieve his desire.

Waiting until the other men had turned away from the table, the young Texian eased back his chair and stood up. Before any of the remaining guests could comment, or question him, he was following the General's party out of the room. None of the five officers became aware of him accompanying them until they were in the office. Urrea went in first, without looking back. Alvarez and Seguin entered in the same fashion. Saucedo however, just before he passed through the door, glanced to his rear. When he realized what he had seen he spun round in anger.

'What the hell are you doing here?' he demanded. 'Get back to the diningroom!'

'I've as much right as you—!' Badillo answered, so surprised by the vehemence of his rival that he took a rapid pace backwards and sent his right hand across to the hilt of his sabre before realizing that the words had not been meant for him.

'You said that I should stay with you, major,' Ole Devil pointed out, ignoring Saucedo as Badillo also looked behind.

While the major had given the young Texian such an instruction on their way to the diningroom, he had not intended it to apply under the present conditions. However, as Ole Devil had hoped, the fact that Saucedo clearly did not want him to attend was sufficient to make Badillo determined to take him in.

'That's what I said,' the major confirmed, starting to walk forward. 'Come on.'

For a moment, Ole Devil thought that the Colonel would repeat the refusal or even attempt to enforce it by physical means. Like the major, Saucedo had a hand on the hilt of his sword and there was an ugly expression on his face. However, hearing voices to his rear, he thought better of it. Letting out a snort of annoyance, he turned on his heel and stalked into the office. Tight lipped and with his whole bearing suggestive of a struggle to control his anger, Badillo followed the colonel. Bringing up the rear, Ole Devil closed the door behind him and stood by it. At first he expected some comment from either Urrea or Alvarez, but neither gave any sign of knowing that he was there. Clearly they were too engrossed in the newcomer to have noticed the young Texian.

'General!' Seguin was saying, as Ole Devil took up his position. 'The Texians have beaten Santa Anna in a battle at the San Jacinto River!'

'So I've already heard,' Urrea grunted.

'He and most of his generals were taken prisoner, along with the majority of their men,' Seguin went on, clearly disappointed to discover that at least part of his news had been anticipated.

'What happened to them?' Urrea asked, slumping into his chair at the desk and waving for the new arrival to be seated at the other side.

Ole Devil for one was pleased with the General's action. It ensured that Seguin was sitting with his back to the door and was therefore unable to see the young Texian.

'Nothing,' the captain admitted. 'Many were killed in the fighting, but those who surrendered haven't been harmed in any way.'

'Not even the senior officers who led the attack on the Alamo, or Santa Anna himself?' Urrea growled, hoping that the information given by "Smithers" might have been incorrect.

'Nobody,' Seguin confirmed. 'That was why I escaped and have ridden relay all the way here. According to a speech made by Santa Anna, he's negotiated with Houston for their return. The way he told it, they'll not only be allowed to leave Texas but are to be given sufficient weapons to ensure their protection.'

Watching from his place by the door, Ole Devil could tell that Alvarez was attaching greater significance to the news than Urrea was. Having assumed his usual position at the General's side, the Paymaster threw a glance pregnant with meaning at him. It was not returned. Clearly Urrea had failed to appreciate the possible implications behind the last piece of information.

How did the prisoners receive the news?' Alvarez asked.

'They were delighted,' Seguin answered. 'I don't think *el Presidente* has been so popular since the start of the campaign. All the men were expecting to be shot and now they're grateful to him for having saved their lives.'

'Did he say why Houston was being so lenient?' the Paymaster inquired.

'Yes,' Seguin confirmed, looking uneasy. To avoid meeting Urrea's eyes, he turned his gaze in Alvarez's direction and went on, 'It was because he'd convinced him that the General had carried out the massacre at Goliad without his authority, then fled to escape the consequences.'

'He did *what?*' Urrea bellowed, hurling back his chair and leaping to his feet.

'Th—That's what he said——!' Seguin insisted, rising in alarm. He had not expected his tidings to be greeted with enthusiasm, but the response was still disconcerting. 'There had already been much ill feeling about the withdrawal of the Tamaulipa Brigade and—and—.'

'Go on, captain,' Alvarez requested gently, setting Urrea's chair on its legs and moving it so that it was pressed against his knees. 'The General is grateful to you for the trouble you have taken and knows you're only repeating what you've heard.'

Combined with the pressure of the chair, the Paymaster's quietly spoken words had the effect of calming Urrea to the point where he was willing to sit down and let the report continue. Sucking in his breath as he too resumed his vacated seat, Seguin explained how there had been an ever growing bitterness against the General and his men for what Santa Anna's troops regarded as their desertion. In fact, it had become accepted that the sole reason for the defeat with such heavy losses had been the absence of the Tamaulipa Brigade.

'Are you saying those sons of whores blame *us* for getting beaten?' Saucedo roared.

'Yes,' Seguin agreed, looking around and, as he was about to continue with his explanation, he noticed Ole

Devil for the first time. 'I'm sure that Santa Anna was behind the—Who's that?'

'I thought, being on Santa Anna's staff, you'd know him,' Saucedo growled with a suggestion of triumph in his voice as he followed the direction of the captain's gaze. 'It's pretty strange that you don't.'

CHAPTER FOURTEEN
Kill The Gringo!

ACCOMPANIED by Tommy Okasi, Mannen Blaze entered the *cantina* which had been established in a large adobe building within the grounds of General José Urrea's *hacienda*. There were a few *vaqueros* and *peons* present, but the majority of the customers were enlisted men serving in the Tamaulipa Lancers or the 'Landero' Line Infantry Battalion. Like their officers, the cavalry-men and the foot soldiers did not mingle. Instead, whether standing at the bar or seated around the tables, they kept to their own kind and paid no attention to each other.

There were a few reasonably pretty Indian and half-breed girls serving or otherwise entertaining the cus-tomers. Behind the counter, assisted by two younger men whose facial resemblances suggested that they might be his sons, a burly Mexican was dispensing drinks.

The *cantina* had been set up at Major Francisco Alvarez's instigation. Being the only source of entertain-ment in the area, it not only provided the soldiers with somewhere to spend their leisure hours, but also extracted the majority of their wages. As the money went to the Paymaster and was then paid back on pay-day, it gave the enlisted men the illusion of receiving wages and kept them reasonably contented without drawing too heavily on Urrea's financial reserves.

Glancing around, Mannen failed to locate Sergeant Moreno or any other member of the escort for Beatriz Alvarez's coach. So he and Tommy made their way towards the space at the counter which separated the Lancers from the infantrymen. All the tables were in use, although there were unoccupied chairs at some of them. However, the Texian considered that it would be advisable to wait until he and Tommy had somebody to vouch for them before coming into close contact even with the Lancers.

Although a number of pairs of eyes were turned towards Mannen and Tommy as they crossed the room, nobody seemed to be showing any special interest in them. Yet, despite the way in which he was dressed, the Texian knew that the soldiers were not mistaking him for a *vaquero*. Unlike Ole Devil Hardin, who had left his hat and pistol in their quarters when he had gone to dinner with the officers, Mannen and Tommy had on their headdress and, apart from the Browning rifle and bow and arrows, were fully armed.

On reaching the bar, Mannen ordered a bottle of wine and two glasses. He had come to the *cantina* on what amounted to a scouting mission. From what he could see, there was little love lost between the horse-and foot-soldiers. The latent hostility was, he concluded, something that Ole Devil might be able to turn to advantage.

Even as the thought came, Mannen was conscious of being watched. Turning to lean with his back to the counter, he swung a sleepy-seeming gaze around the room. None of the crowd appeared to be paying more than casual attention to him. Nor, with the burly bartender standing so close and possibly able to understand English, could he discuss the matter with Tommy. A glance at the little Oriental showed that he too had

165

been studying their surroundings. As their eyes met, Tommy gave a quick shake of his head that suggested he had found nothing to alarm him.

For all that, danger was threatening the Texian and his companion.

Seated at a table with several members of his Company, a heavily built and hard-faced infantry sergeant was giving instructions to his men. Word had been passed down to the Battalion's non-coms that their commanding officer had no liking for the *gringos* and 'Indian' who had arrived that afternoon. In fact, providing that it could be made to appear that they were at fault, Colonel Sebastian Saucedo would not be averse to them being killed or seriously injured. With the proviso in mind, the sergeant was hatching a plot. About five minutes later, he saw his opportunity to put it into operation.

An Indian girl carrying a loaded tray was approaching the sergeant's table. Waiting until she was close enough, he rose. Bumping into her, he contrived to knock the tray so that the drinks were spilled over his uniform.

'You stupid whore!' the sergeant roared, and swung a slap to the girl's face. It sent her staggering and, following, he caught her by the hair and dress. With a heave, he flung her across the room to land almost at Mannen's feet. Stalking forward, he went on, 'I'll teach you to be so damned clumsy.'

Although the incident was attracting a lot of attention, none of the Mexicans offered to intervene. Behind the bar, the manager let out a grunt of what might have been protest. However, knowing the sergeant to be a dangerous proposition, he was disinclined to divert the wrath from the Indian girl to himself. Nor did he expect anybody else to take the girl's part.

'That's enough!' Mannen said quietly, stepping over the girl.

166

'What the hell has it got to do with you, *gringo*?' the sergeant demanded, coming to a halt as the Texian confronted him.

'Looked to me as if the fault was yours, not the girl's,' Mannen answered. 'Leave her be.'

Even as he was speaking, the young Texian realized that he might have acted in an unwise manner. However, his instincts and upbringing would not have allowed him to stand back while a member of the opposite sex was being abused. It was, he concluded, too late to have second thoughts. Having intervened, he must carry the matter through to its conclusion.

For his part, the sergeant was very satisfied with the way things were turning out. He had heard that *gringos* were soft-hearted and protective where women were concerned and had based his strategy upon it. Few, if any, of the non-com's section of Mexican society would have offered to protect an Indian girl, but he had hoped that the *gringo* would. Now he had an acceptable excuse for attacking the sleepy-looking young Texian. Nor did he anticipate any great danger. The greatest risk was that some of the Lancers might take the *gringo's* side, but none of them were showing any sign of it. Even if they did, the sergeant felt confident that the members of his regiment who were present would support him.

Behind the counter, the *cantina's* manager glanced at his elder son and gave a jerk of his head. Without needing any verbal command, the young man went through the door which gave access to the rear of the building. Showing no sign of being aware of his son's departure, the manager turned his attention to what was happening on the other side of the bar. However, he neither spoke nor made any attempt to interfere.

'Get out of my way, *gringo*!' the sergeant ordered, taking a step forward. His right hand went behind him to the hilt of the knife sheathed on the back of his belt.

Instantly, the non-com discovered—as Moreno had at the *Posada del Madonna*—that the Texian's slothful appearance was deceptive. Moving with an unexpected speed, Mannen swung his right arm in a cuff to the side of the sergeant's head. Such was the force behind the open handed blow that its recipient was spun around and sent reeling in the direction from which he had come. Seeing him rushing towards them without any control over his movements, the men who had shared his table shoved back their chairs and started to stand up. Unable to stop himself, the sergeant struck the table. It crumpled under his weight, depositing him on the floor along with two of his companions who had not moved quickly enough.

Furious curses sounded, mingling with the far from tactful laughter of the Lancers. More chairs clattered over as a number of infantrymen came to their feet. The were mostly sergeants and corporals who were aware of Saucedo's wishes regarding the Texians. Guessing what the recipient of Mannen's blow had hoped to achieve, they intended to carry on where he had inadvertently left off.

'Kill the *gringo*!' yelled one of the sergeants. 'Get the "Indian" too!'

Hands went to the hilts of the Baker bayonets which swung in the frogs on several of the foot soldiers' belts. Others reached for the knives which they carried.

If Tommy had been granted an opportunity, he would have advised Mannen against interfering between the Mexican and the girl. He had sensed that it might be a trap, but had had no chance of speaking. However, he drew the correct conclusion when he heard the second sergeant's shouted command, deducing from the word '*Indio*' that he too was to be made a victim of reprisals.

Even as the Mexicans were starting to draw their weapons, Tommy stepped to Mannen's right side. Although the Texian had not made a move towards

168

either his pistol or bowie knife, the little Oriental slid the thirty inch long blade of the *tachi* sword from its sheath. Grasping the handle in both hands, Tommy adopted the traditional *Samurai* warrior's on-guard posture.

'All right,' Mannen said, his voice raised sufficiently to carry all around the suddenly silent room. 'We didn't come in here to look for trouble and, so there won't be any, we'll leave.'

Starting to move forward, with his long bayonet held ready for use, the second sergeant noticed a certain hesitancy among his companions. Nor did he feel as confident of success as he had previously. There was something grimly menacing about the two young men which was causing their would-be attackers to have second thoughts. Nor was it solely due to the naked blade in Tommy's hands. While Mannen had not yet offered to draw a weapon, he had lost much of his lethargic appearance. The way in which he had felled the first non-com was proof that he was far from being as slow as he looked. In fact, the infantrymen felt sure that he would be a fast and dangerous antagonist.

If there had only been members of his own Battalion present, the sergeant might have felt inclined to accept the big Texian's offer. He could have waited for a more suitable opportunity to carry out Saucedo's instructions. However, with the weight of numbers so heavily in his favour and, moreover, the fact that he was being watched by many of the Lancers, made him decide not to back down.

'Like hell you will!' the non-com snarled. 'Come on, let's get the——!'

'Hey, *amigo*,' called a voice which Mannen recognized. 'It looks like *you* need help this time.'

Glancing across the room, the Texian found that he had made a correct identification of the speaker. Sergeant Moreno and an Indian-dark, grim looking Lancers' sergeant major had come through the side door. Followed by the rest of Beatriz's escort, they advanced until they formed a rough half circle around Mannen and Tommy.

While crossing the room, Sergeant Major Gomez had looked from the Indian girl as she crouched on the floor, with blood running from the corner of her mouth, to the non-com who was still sprawled supine on the ruined table. Guessing what the sight implied, he swung his gaze to the second sergeant. Under normal circumstances, Gomez would have been indifferent to the mistreatment of the Indian girl. Nor would he have been unduly perturbed by the idea of the foot soldiers assaulting and at least seriously injuring the *gringo* and his companion. However, Major Carlos Badillo had made his sentiments known regarding the latter and Gomez intended to see that they were respected.

'What's happened?' the sergeant major demanded, although he could have hazarded a guess at the answer.

'I don't see how it comes to be any of *your* business,' the infantry sergeant replied truculently. 'It's between us and those two. So you'd better step aside and keep out of things that don't concern you.'

'These men are *my* concern,' Gomez stated, having received orders from Badillo regarding the safety of the two *gringos* and their Indian. On top of that, he disliked the infantry sergeant's attitude. 'General Urrea has said that they can enlist in the Tamaulipa Lancers, so I don't intend to let anything happen to them.'

'Did you hear that, *amigos*?' the sergeant shouted, looking at the seated infantrymen with the intention of enlisting their support. He had always resented having to walk while the Lancers rode. Nor had their attitude of superiority ever sat well with him. 'These damned horse-soldiers have had to start taking on *gringos* to do their fighting for them.'

'Any time you stinking foot-shufflers feel like trying to

see how much help we need to fight,' Gomez answered. 'Just say the word and we'll show you.'

There was a scraping of chairs' legs on the floor and a low, angry rumbling of talk, as members of both regiments began to stand up. The hostility which existed between their respective commanding officers had been passed down to them, increasing the traditional rivalry between their branches of the service. So they were eager to try conclusions with one another. Nor, from what Mannen Blaze could see, would the matter be settled with just fists and a rough-house brawl. Every right hand was reaching for a weapon as the Lancers and the infantrymen formed into two groups on opposite sides of the barroom.

*   *   *   *   *

After Colonel Sebastian Saucedo had finished speaking, he and all the other officers in General José Urrea's office turned their eyes in Ole Devil Hardin's direction. The young Texian could sense that the words had started to arouse doubts, even suspicion, regarding his story about having been close to *Presidente* Antonio Lopez de Santa Anna.

Ole Devil had realized that there was a danger of his identity being challenged if he attempted to find out what news had been brought by Captain Seguin, but he had felt it was a risk he must take. Up until Saucedo had drawn the newcomer's attention to him, he had been congratulating himself on having made the right decision. It had confirmed his conclusion that he was not the reason for Seguin's arrival. If he had been, the captain would have looked for and denounced him. In addition, he had gathered some information that he might be able to turn to his advantage. Provided, of course, that he could clear himself of suspicion.

'I'd be surprised if the captain did know me,' Ole Devil declared, walking forward with an air of nonchalance which appeared to suggest he had nothing to fear. He

171

was directing his words straight at Saucedo, and his attitude implied that the colonel was the only person present who needed convincing of his *bona-fides*. 'Or do *you* think that *el Presidente* used to go around telling everybody I was a spy he'd hired to keep an eye on them?'

'It doesn't seem likely to me that he would,' Major Carlos Badillo remarked, doing what the Texian had hoped that he would. Despite the uncertainty which had been aroused by Saucedo's comment, he could not resist opposing and trying to show up his rival. 'Surely that would tend to restrict the spy's effectiveness.'

'Did you ever see this man?' the colonel insisted, ignoring the major's sarcastic words and pointing a finger at Ole Devil.

Although the captain looked at the Texian, he did not immediately reply. Seguin was on the horns of a dilemma, and he did not care for the sensation. While the *gringo* seemed vaguely familiar, the captain was unable to decide whether he had seen him before or not. Nor, in view of the way in which Saucedo and Badillo were staring at him, did he relish the idea of making an answer. Wanting to remain in Urrea's service, he had no desire to antagonize either officer. Both, he knew, were very influential in the Tamaulipa Brigade. Saucedo might be the senior in rank, but the captain was a cavalryman and as such would probably be put in the Lancers under Badillo's command. Even if he should be retained on the General's staff, whoever he went against would remember and be his enemy.

'Well, captain,' Major Francisco Alvarez put in mildly, after about thirty seconds had elapsed without a reply. 'Have you seen this young man or not?'

'I—I—,' Seguin began, shifting uneasily on his chair and trying to avoid meeting anybody's eyes.

'I wasn't dressed this way in those days, captain and, as I had a beard and moustache, you might not recognize me,' Ole Devil put in, halting alongside Seguin and speaking in a friendly manner, guessing what was causing the other's perturbation. 'On top of which, as *el Presidente* didn't want it suspected that I was spying for him, Major Fuqua always arranged for us to meet after dark and in secret.'

Watching the Paymaster rather than any of the others, the Texian sensed that the final point he had raised was working strongly in his favour. Amongst other information which he had been given before leaving on his mission, was the identity of the officer who would have handled dealings between Santa Anna and a man such as he was pretending to be. Clearly Alvarez, for one, was aware of the kind of duties that Major Fuqua— ostensibly a mere quartermaster—actually carried out.

'Well, I—,' Seguin spluttered, still not wanting to have to commit himself either way. Then he saw how the *gringo's* explanation could be used as an excuse for avoiding the issue. 'I could have seen him, but don't recognize him. As an officer and a gentleman, I never approved of using renegades and didn't have anything to do with them. So I can't say for sure———.'

A knock on the door brought the captain's words to a stop. It opened and Saucedo's second-in-command entered, followed by a worried-looking young civilian.

'My apologies, *senores*,' the major said, indicating his companion with a jerk of his right thumb. 'Esteban's sent his son to tell Alvarez that there could be trouble at the *cantina*.'

'Why should he send for you, Francisco?' Urrea demanded. 'It's the officer—.'

'I told Esteban to notify *me* immediately if it seemed likely that there would be trouble,' the Paymaster interrupted. 'There's been considerable friction between the two regiments recently and I felt it was advisable that we heard about any trouble 'as soon as possible so that we could get there and prevent it from developing into anything more serious.'

"What kind of trouble might it be?' Saucedo barked at his second-in-command.

'We'd better go over and find out,' Alvarez advised, giving the major no time to reply and starting to walk around the desk. 'If the trouble-makers see us it will have a greater calming effect than just sending the officer-of-the-day.'

'It will,' Urrea conceded and lurched to his feet. 'Come on, all of you.'

'I don't think we need Captain Seguin with us, General,' Alvarez pointed out. 'He has had a long, hard journey and looks as if he could use a good meal.'

'You'd better go and get one,' Urrea authorized as he strode by the man in question.

'Stay here and I'll have food sent in to you, captain,' Alvarez ordered. 'It'd be as well if the news you've brought us doesn't go any farther. So, if you should be questioned, just say you've come to tell the General about Santa Anna losing the battle. 'Don't mention the rest of it.'

Following the Mexicans as they hurried from the office, Ole Devil was both pleased and perturbed by the interruption. It had won him a respite from a very tricky situation, for which he was grateful. While Seguin had failed to expose him as an impostor, neither had he received a clean bill of health. If the interrogation had continued, somebody was almost certain to have asked the captain whether he had heard of 'Count von Richthofen' and it was a name he would be unlikely to forget. In fact, Ole Devil had expected Alvarez to do so even if it had not occurred to any of the others.

Dampening Ole Devil's relief was the knowledge that Mannen Blaze and Tommy Okasi had said that they would visit the *cantina* to see what they could learn. Trouble there might easily involve them.

174

'Huh!' Urrea snorted, leading the way through the side door nearest to the *cantina*. 'Everything's quiet enough!'

'Too quiet!' Alvarez answered, studying the well-lit and silent building. 'Come on, we may still be in time!'

The urgency in the Paymaster's tone caused the men with him to move even faster. Striding out with greater alacrity than he usually employed, Urrea was the first to reach the *cantina*. What he saw through one of the windows told him that Alvarez had acted with customary forethought and had made a wise decision in making the arrangement with Esteban. Nor had they been summoned by a false alarm. Although the members of the two regiments had not yet come to grips, they were facing each other and were clearly on the point of commencing hostilities.

To give Urrea his due, he did not hesitate. Kicking open the *cantina's* front door, he passed through it with a bellow that brought every eye to him. Finding themselves in the presence of their commanding general and other senior officers, the Lancers and the infantrymen allowed their weapons to sag into less threatening positions. Showing as great a speed as when producing his *tachi*, Tommy returned it to its sheath. Mannen removed his hand from the hilt of the still undrawn bowie knife and adopted an attitude of half asleep innocence.

'Put those knives and bayonets away!' Urrea bellowed and, after the order had been reluctantly obeyed, went on, 'What's been happening here?'

'The Lancers——!' the sergeant from Saucedo's battalion began.

'Those Infantry——!' Gomez commenced at the same instant.

'Quiet!' Urrea bellowed as the non-coms stopped speaking to glare at each other and a low, ominous rumble arose among their supporters.

Although silence fell, the ugly way in which the two

175

groups continued to glare at each other made it seem no less menacing than it had been before.

'Might I suggest that we send the men back to their lines, General?' Alvarez asked.

'Yes,' Urrea agreed. 'The *cantina's* closed. Get back to your lines.'

'It would be advisable for the officers to accompany them,' the Paymaster went on. 'In fact, it would be better if they spend the night with their men. That will keep them apart until their tempers have had time to cool down and it will ensure there are no further incidents.'

'See to it, Colonel Saucedo, Major Badillo!' Urrea commanded. 'Report to me in the morning and tell me the cause of all this.'

Standing just inside the front door, Ole Devil was not dissatisfied by the way things had turned out. In addition to there being a rift between Urrea's two regiments which would take a lot of healing, the matter of his connection with Santa Anna had been postponed and, with the latest development demanding attention, might even be forgotten.

CHAPTER FIFTEEN
A Wise Man Knows When To Get Out

BEFORE Ole Devil Hardin had taken two steps through the door of General José Urrea's office, he sensed that something was wrong. It showed in the attitudes of the room's other occupants. Colonel Sebastian Saucedo was glowering at him from the right side of the desk with mingled hatred and thinly veiled satisfaction. At the other end, Major Carlos Badillo threw a speculative glance at the young Texian and then resumed scowling at his rival. Seated in his usual chair, Urrea was studying Ole Devil with a cold and suspicious gaze. Although nothing showed on the lean, aesthetic face, Major Francisco Alvarez was looking at him just as fixedly.

Puzzled by his reception, Ole Devil noticed that Captain Seguin was not present. So he assumed that the order to report to Urrea's office had nothing to do with the challenge to his identity. Most probably he had been summoned to account for the part played by Mannen Blaze and Tommy Okasi in the previous night's disturbance at the *cantina*.

Waiting until Saucedo and Badillo had left with their respective groups of enlisted men, Alvarez had suggested to Urrea that any inquiry into the affair should be put off until the following morning. Accepting the advice, the General had told Ole Devil to take his two companions to their quarters and keep them there. Wanting to know what had happened, Ole Devil had been only too willing to obey.

On reaching the comparative privacy of their room and talking in whispers, Ole Devil, his cousin, and the little Oriental had discussed and drawn conclusions from the incident. Then, Ole Devil had told the other two of the latest developments on his side. While agreeing that Seguin's arrival had added to the danger of their mission, they had realized that leaving was out of the question. If they were caught trying to escape, it would be regarded as proof that they were not what they pretended to be. So, knowing that they had no other alternative, they had accepted that they must stay at the *hacienda* and bluff things out until presented with an opportunity to do their work and get away. Having reached their decision, they had gone to bed and slept until morning.

'What did you do after you left the *cantina* last night, *Senor* Smithers?' Urrea inquired, as the Texian came to a halt in a smart military brace on the opposite side of the desk. The suspicious look did not leave his face but he was clearly pleased by the other's respectful attitude.

'I took my men to our quarters, as *you* ordered, *patrón*,' Ole Devil replied, wondering if the conversation he had had with Mannen and Tommy could have been overheard.

'And none of you left it?' the General went on.

'*You'd* told us to stay there, *patrón*,' Ole Devil pointed out, his manner suggesting that he considered such an order must be obeyed unhesitatingly. 'Is there some reason for you to think that we might not have obeyed your order?'

'A very good one,' Saucedo put in. 'This morning Captain Seguin was found in his room with his throat cut.'

'And I've been accused of doing it,' Ole Devil guessed, addressing the words to Urrea without even so much as glancing at the colonel.

'Who else would have had reason for killing him?' Saucedo demanded, goaded on by the way the Texian appeared to be ignoring him. 'Seguin was on Santa Anna's staff—.'

'And could have proved who I was,' Ole Devil interrupted.

'Or who you're not!' Saucedo countered. 'Nobody else had a reason to kill him.'

'How about somebody who'd been spying for Santa Anna and was frightened that Seguin might expose him?' Ole Devil inquired and, turning his gaze to the colonel, continued, 'Or it could have been *somebody* who didn't want him to say he recognized me and I'm who I claim to be.'

'Who'd do it for *that* reason?' Badillo asked, but this attitude showed that he could have supplied the answer.

'There's only one person here who hasn't accepted me,' Ole Devil replied, swinging his eyes back to Urrea. 'Even though *you* are satisfied, General—.'

'You god-damned *gringo* son-of-a-whore!' Saucedo bellowed, seeing how Urrea might regard such a suggestion. His right hand went to the hilt of his sword. 'Are you saying that I——.'

'You're the only one who isn't satisfied with him,' Badillo put in, once again playing the game as Ole Devil had hoped he would. He could see how the Texian's comment might be used to put the colonel in the wrong with their superior. 'So——.'

'Gentlemen!' Alvarez barked and something in his voice caused the two officers to freeze instead of drawing their weapons. 'Arguing among ourselves won't settle anything——.'

'Damn it!' Saucedo snarled, although the Paymaster had clearly been meaning to say more. 'He accused me——.'

'All I did was point out two other possibilities, *patrón*,' Ole Devil protested. 'I admit that I seem the most likely suspect. But, even if I'd need to silence Seguin, how would I have known where to find him. I never saw him after we went to the cantina and I still don't know which room he was using.'

'Neither did I!' Saucedo pointed out. 'I spent the night with my men and didn't come back here until this morning. You were in the house.'

'That's true, colonel,' Alvarez put in. 'But he couldn't have left his quarters. I took the precaution of having a watch kept on his door and window. There was no way he could have got out and back without being seen.'

'Which means *he* couldn't have killed Seguin,' Badillo stated, putting an emphasis on the third word and turning his gaze from the Texian, he went on, 'So *somebody* else must have!'

The way in which the final sentence was said caused Urrea to follow the direction of the major's gaze, an action duplicated by Ole Devil and Alvarez. Finding himself the object of their combined scrutiny, Saucedo stiffened and a flush of anger darkened his far from pleasant features.

"God damn it!' the colonel roared, and resumed the drawing of his sword. 'If you're saying *I* killed him!'

'Stop that, both of you!' Urrea bellowed, rising with such alacrity that he sent his chair flying as Badillo began to slide free the sabre's blade. 'Sheath those swords immediately.'

At first, Ole Devil thought that the two men would refuse to obey. Saucedo was close to homicidal rage, and Badillo showed just as great a willingness to confront him. A good thirty seconds went by before the major, giving a mocking smile, thrust down the sabre and stiffened to a position of attention with his right hand clear of the hilt. Scowling, and with every evidence of bad grace, Saucedo complied with the command a few seconds later. In spite of their obedience, they continued to keep a wary eye on each other. It was obvious that, as far as they were concerned, the incident was far from over.

'*Patrón*,' Ole Devil said, still standing as stiff as a ramrod despite being between the two officers. 'As my presence in *your* service appears to be an embarassment, perhaps I and my men should move on.'

'I don't see why they should have to, General,' Badillo protested, looking defiantly at Saucedo. 'They're useful fighting men and they weren't to blame for the trouble at the *cantina* last night.'

'Are you saying *my* men were?' the colonel challenged.

'This is getting us nowhere!' Alvarez put in. 'I'd suggest, General, that Colonel Saucedo and Major Badillo rejoin their commands to ensure that there are no further incidents between them——.'

'How about Seguin?' Saucedo demanded. 'Damn it, I've been accused——.'

'No accusation has been made, colonel,' Alvarez interrupted. 'And, with the General's permission, I will con-

180

duct an investigation to see if I can find out who did kill him.'

'Do that, Francisco,' Urrea authorized. 'And I want you two to stay with your regiments until I give other orders.'

'It would be advisable for *Senor* Smithers and his men to stay here in the *hacienda*,' Alvarez remarked, before either officer could respond.

'I thought you were sure they couldn't have done it,' the colonel sneered.

'*I'm* satisfied that they couldn't have!' Urrea stated, drawing a bitter scowl from Saucedo.

'All the evidence certainly points that way, colonel,' the Paymaster went on. 'But your men might regard them as a source of provocation if they are with the Lancers.'

'You'll find the Lancers can take care of their own,' Badillo declared, oozing provocative arrogance. 'Of course, not all troops are as well disciplined—.'

'Some of them are trained for fighting, not to act like dressed-up popinjays,' Saucedo snarled. 'And in Texas—.'

'That's enough!' Urrea shouted. 'You'll leave first, major. Go straight to your regiment's lines and stay there until I send for you. That applies to you also, Colonel Saucedo.'

Once again there was a distinct hesitation before the order was obeyed. Observing the way the colonel and the major were glaring at each other, Ole Devil expected Alvarez to try and lessen their hostility. Even if Urrea did not see the danger, the Paymaster was intelligent enough to appreciate how the two officers' bitter emnity was likely to weaken their fighting force at a time when it needed to be at its full strength. However, Alvarez neither spoke nor moved.

Snapping tighter into his brace, Badillo threw a salute to the General and stalked from the office. The stiff-backed manner in which he took his departure sug-

181

gested that he was far from pleased by the way in which he had been dismissed and the orders he had received.

Glowering after the departing major, Saucedo swung his gaze to Urrea and opened his mouth. Before he could speak, the General turned and went to pick up the chair. It was, Ole Devil decided, anything but diplomatic and tactful behaviour. Closing his lips into a tight line with the words unsaid, the colonel turned his eyes to Alvarez. Instead of trying to relieve the situation, the Paymaster returned the gaze with stony indifference. So, flinging a look redolent of deepest hatred at the Texian, Saucedo stamped across the room. If the way in which he slammed the door behind him was anything to go by, he was highly dissatisfied with his treatment.

Placing his chair at the desk, Urrea glared indignantly at the door. He seemed on the point of calling Saucedo back, but thought better of it.

'I don't think he killed Seguin, Francisco,' the General said, but his voice showed doubt. 'Do you?'

'There's no reason why he should have,' the Paymaster answered. 'I'll start my investigation and see what I can find out.'

'*Bueno*!' Urrea grunted, having made no attempt to sit down. 'Is there anything more you need me for?'

'No,' Alvarez replied.

'Then I'm going up to my quarters for a while,' Urrea declared. 'You needn't send for me unless something comes up that you can't handle by yourself.'

If Ole Devil had had any doubts of how things stood between the Paymaster and the General, they were now resolved. An expression of disdain and loathing came briefly to Alvarez's face as he watched Urrea crossing to the door. It confirmed all the young Texian's suspicions.

'Have you any orders for me, major?' Ole Devil inquired, after the General had left the office and the Paymaster showed no signs of following him.

'I want a talk with you,' Alvarez answered, going to Urrea's chair. Although his features had resumed their usual expression, to the Texian there was something symbolic in the way he sat down. His attitude was that of a man who had finally taken his rightful place. 'What do you think of General Urrea now that you've met him, *Senor*—Smithers?'

'That he's *very* fortunate to have such a sound adviser to do his thinking and guide him,' Ole Devil answered, putting his conclusions to the test.

'How do you mean?' the Paymaster said quietly, almost mildly, but without any puzzlement in his tone.

'I know who the real brains of the Tamaulipa Brigade is,' Ole Devil stated. 'And it *isn't* General José Urrea.'

'In that case may I ask who it is?'

'*You* don't need to, major. It shows in the way he always looks to *you* before he makes a decision and in how *you* keep "advising" and "suggesting" things to him so that he doesn't say or do the wrong thing.'

'What do you think of the situation in the light of the news brought by Seguin?' Alvarez wanted to know and, try as he might, he could not entirely hide his pleasure at having received such a tribute from a young man whose intelligence he held in high regard.

'Pretty much the same as you,' Ole Devil replied without hesitation. 'And any slight chance Urrea had of becoming *Presidente* in spite of the news has been ruined by the hostility between the two regiments. And he hasn't done anything to improve matters by taking my side against Saucedo.'

'Go on,' the Paymaster prompted.

'I'd guess that there was bad blood between Badillo and Saucedo even before we arrived,' Ole Devil obliged.

'You *did* guess and played them off against each other,' Alvarez corrected. 'As you said, though, there's always been bad blood between them and they passed it down to their men during the campaign despite the fact that I tried to stop it. Being mounted, the Lancers could almost always arrive at their objective first and so got the cream of the loot. That always annoyed the infantry men. Colonel Ortega was able to prevent the ill feeling from getting out of hand and might still have been able to settle their differences. But, although I'm the only one who's seen it, a message arrived from him last night. He says that he's resigning from the army because of continued bad health and won't be coming back.'

'Which puts Badillo in command of the Lancers,' Ole Devil finished. 'And makes me even more certain that Urrea hasn't a hope of becoming *Presidente*. Saucedo will never co-operate with Badillo.'

'And what other conclusions have you drawn?'

'As a guess, the same that you have. A wise man knows when to get out. Which's why I offered to leave just now.'

'Where would you go?' Alvarez inquired. 'Sit down if you wish.'

'*Gracias*,' Ole Devil answered and moved along until he could hook his rump on to the edge of the desk. As he did so, he noticed that the Paymaster had opened a drawer and was sitting with his right hand inside it. 'You've hit my biggest problem. I wouldn't want to show my face in Texas——.'

'I wonder just how unsafe *that* might be?' the Paymaster remarked.

Silence fell!

For almost a minute, Ole Devil and Alvarez studied each other like duellists awaiting the signal to start fighting, even though outwardly nothing in the office had changed. Showing no sign of placing any significance on the words, Ole Devil continued to lounge on the edge of the desk. Alvarez looked more like a monk engrossed in spiritual meditation than a man who was participating in a battle of wits with a shrewd and capable antagonist.

'Just what did Seguin tell you, major?' the Texian said at last, deciding that attack might be his best form of defense. 'Before *you* killed him.'

'Before *I* killed him?' Alvarez responded placidly, but he stiffened just a trifle and his eyes took on a wary, steel-hard glint.

'It has to be,' Ole Devil declared, tense and ready to take any action that might become necessary. He had a pretty good idea of why the Paymaster's hand was in the drawer. 'I didn't, and no matter how I made it look, Saucedo wouldn't have had enough imagination to do it just to incriminate and get rid of me.'

'You suggested another alternative to Urrea,' Alvarez pointed out.

'If Seguin had come to expose one of Santa Anna's spies, he'd never have let the man into his room. No, major, you're the only other possibility. You assigned him to his quarters, so you knew where to find him. If he was as fooled as most people by your pose, he wouldn't hesitate to let you in; even assuming that you didn't kill him as soon as you'd taken him in and questioned him about me.'

'And why should *I* kill him?'

'To put *me* in a position where I'll have to go along with any proposition that you make to me,' Ole Devil replied, and sensed that he was correct, although there was little enough visible evidence of it on the Paymaster's face. 'Come on, major. Let's put our cards on the table. You still don't know any more about me than you did before you had your last talk with Seguin.'

'That's true,' Alvarez admitted. 'He said that he'd never heard of you as "Count von Richthofen" or "*Senor*" Smithers, but put it down to having had no dealings at all with renegades or taken any interest in what they did.'

'There weren't many regular officers who approved of us renegades,' Ole Devil commented. 'Which's why *el*

185

Presidente gave us those passes. But that's beside the point. He might not have cleared things up about me, but he told you enough of what was happening in Texas for you to feel sure that Urrea can't become *Presidente*.'

'He did,' the Paymaster agreed. 'Santa Anna is going to smash Urrea as the first step towards staying in power, to prove to anybody else who might object that he's still a force to be reckoned with. And, with Saucedo and Badillo at each other's throats, he could do it.'

'So you decided that the time had come to quit,' Ole Devil guessed. 'And, needing an escort, you want me to supply it with my cousin and our multi-shot rifles.'

'That's correct,' Alvarez confirmed.

'What's in it for me?' Ole Devil asked.

'You're hardly in a position to bargain,' Alvarez warned. 'All I have to do is "find out" that one of the men I had watching you fell asleep for long enough to let you leave, kill Seguin and return.'

'Except that I'd tell Urrea what you've said and how you intend to bolt,' Ole Devil countered.

'You might not find that easy to do——,' the Paymaster began, starting to bring his hand from the drawer.

Instantly Ole Devil slipped from the desk. Before his feet met the floor, he was in the process of arming himself, thankful that he had donned the Manton pistol that morning. Using all the speed he could muster, he began to twist the weapon from its belt loop.

Swiftly as the Texian was moving, Alvarez was similarly rapid. He lifted a flintlock pistol out of the drawer. The two muzzles turned into alignment simultaneously.

There was, however, one vitally important difference!

Following his usual procedure, Ole Devil cocked his weapon while making the draw. About to pull back the flintlock's hammer, Alvarez heard the clicking of the other pistol's mechanism and refrained from doing so.

'Why get killed, major?' Ole Devil challenged. 'It won't do either of us any good.'

'I suppose not,' the Paymaster conceded, returning the pistol and closing the drawer. 'Shall we talk business?'

'That's what I wanted to do all along,' Ole Devil declared, lowering the Manton's hammer to half-cock then placing it in its loop. 'What do you have in mind?'

'To get out of Mexico,' Alvarez explained. 'So I want you and your men to escort us as far as Vera Cruz where we can take a ship to Spain.'

'Going there will take money,' Ole Devil pointed out. 'Not that I think you and your wife don't have any. In fact, I'd say you'll have enough to be pretty well fixed when you arrive.'

'I won't insult your intelligence by denying it,' Alvarez promised. 'And I'm willing to make it worth your while to escort us.'

'Well now, major, that's going to be a long journey. Sure we'll be moving ahead of Santa Anna and will reach Vera Cruz before he's anywhere near. But, while you're safe on the seas, I'll have to come back.'

'Why should you come back?'

'I don't intend to spend the rest of my life in Mexico, and it's not likely I'll be able to get a ship back to the United States.'

'You said that you daren't go back there,' Alvarez pointed out.

'Not to Louisiana,' Ole Devil corrected. 'But there's a lot of land up north where I could get a fresh start. Except that to do it, I'll need money.'

'I've told you that I'll pay you,' Alvarez answered.

'Mexican *pesos* aren't a whole lot of use up in the United States,' Ole Devil pointed out. 'All I'm interested in is good old U.S. dollars.'

'I can get them through my banker in Vera Cruz,' Alvarez offered.

'What guarantee do I have that you'll do it?' Ole Devil countered.

'What guarantee do I have that you'll keep your end of the bargain if I should make a payment in advance?'

'Could you?'

'I could, having gathered some U.S. dollars during the campaign in Texas,' Alvarez replied. 'So I'll give you—two hundred and fifty—now, and arrange for the same sum on our arrival.'

'Make it five hundred in advance and another thousand on arrival and you've hired yourself a man,' Ole Devil suggested. 'I wouldn't do it for less.'

'Very well,' Alvarez sighed. 'You drive a hard bargain, but I have to go.'

'We'll need enough *pesos* to pay our way back to Texas, too,' Ole Devil went on.

'Can you wait for them until we reach Vera Cruz?'

'Sure, major. When do you want to start?'

'This afternoon,' the Paymaster replied. 'I want to be on my way shortly after four o'clock. So be at the stables with your horses saddled by then. Our coach will be loaded and ready. We'll join you there.'

'How will you explain to Urrea about us going away?' Ole Devil inquired.

'Leave that to me,' Alvarez replied. 'I'll promise you that he won't interfere. Nor will Badillo and Saucedo, they'll have other things on their minds.'

With that, the Paymaster came to his feet. His attitude showed that the matter was settled as far as he was concerned. When Ole Devil attempted to prolong the discussion and gather further information. Alvarez resisted on the grounds that there was already little enough time left to complete all the preparations for their departure. Ole Devil pointed out that they had not yet decided upon the sum he would receive in *pesos* and, after a short exchange of bargaining, they reached an agreement. Leaving the office, they went their separate ways.

Going to his room, Ole Devil told Mannen and Tommy of the latest developments and the conclusions

188

he had drawn. After which, they started to get ready for making their departure.

'How did it go, 'Cisco?' Beatriz Alvarez wanted to know, as her husband joined her in their suite.

'Just as we planned,' the Paymaster replied.

'Will the *gringos* escort us?' Beatriz inquired, knowing that her husband was counting on Ole Devil, Mannen and Tommy—backed by the repeating rifles—to provide a more effective protection than would be offered by any of the men on his staff who could be trusted.

'Yes,' the Paymaster confirmed, a mocking smile playing on his lips. 'For a price.'

'How much?'

'I've promised "Smithers" fifteen hundred dollars and a thousand *pesos* to cover their expenses on the way back from Vera Cruz to the *Rio Bravo*.'

'You're very generous, my husband,' Beatriz purred.

'I can afford to be,' Alvarez answered. 'After all, they won't live long enough to collect the money.'

CHAPTER SIXTEEN
Now I'll Have To Kill You

BEATRIZ ALVAREZ gave a well simulated shriek of alarm and sprang away from Major Carlos Badillo, staring at Colonel Sebastian Saucedo who, sword in hand, was stepping into view from behind a clump of bushes. Seeing his rival's head turn in his direction, the burly officer spat out a curse and started to rush forward. Instead of offering to explain his presence, or asking what had brought the other man to the clearing in the woodland about half a mile south of General José Urrea's *hacienda*, Badillo began to snatch the sabre from its sheath so that he could defend himself against the colonel's attack.

Although the woman could have told the two officers that the situation was not what they imagined, she had no intention of doing so. Nor was it likely that either of them would have listened to her. Their mutual hatred, long festering and growing, had been brought to a head and was filling them with an irresistible desire to kill. It was so compelling that neither suspected they had been manipulated into the present situation for Major Francisco Alvarez's purposes.

Saucedo's arrival was in response to a message from Beatriz, saying that Badillo had learned of their relationship and was threatening to tell her husband. Approaching the clearing where she had asked him to meet her, he had seen that the major was already there. Deciding that it would be an ideal opportunity to kill his rival, he drew his sword and moved in quietly. His hope of taking Badillo by surprise had failed due to what he imagined was the woman's inadvertent response on seeing him. It did not occur to him that, having asked him to meet her in the clearing at half past three, she ought not to have been surprised when he appeared.

Having been lured by a similar message, Badillo was no more aware than Saucedo of Beatriz's treachery. Nor, under the circumstances, could he devote time to wondering how the colonel came to be on the spot at such an inopportune moment. His thoughts were entirely occupied with how he could save his own life and kill Saucedo.

Much the better fencer, Badillo was not given the opportunity to make full use of his superior skill. Even as his sabre came free from the scabbard, Saucedo was almost upon him.

Up swung the colonel's right arm, so as to deliver a

blow that would end the matter to his satisfaction. Before it could be completed, Badillo went into a classic lunge. Flashing forward, the point of the sabre sank deep into the left side of Saucedo's breast. Mortal though the thrust was, it came too late to prevent the colonel's sword from descending. Down it whipped, driven by all the power in his body. At almost the same instant that Badillo's weapon pierced Saucedo's heart, his blade struck the top of the major's skull and split it open to the bridge of the nose.

Both men went down, killed instantly, victims of the kind of reckless attack which the French called the *coup des deux veuves.** They died without discovering how, or why, they had been tricked.

Looking down at the corpses for a moment, Beatriz swung on her heel and walked rapidly away. Revulsion and horror over what had happened was not the cause of her retreat. Although she had pretended affection for each of them—and had been much more intimate in her dealings with them than her husband suspected—their deaths meant nothing to her. No matter how far she had gone in love-making, her relationships had been no more than a means to serve Alvarez's ends.

Having seen the first part of her husband's latest scheme brought to a much more successful conclusion than they had anticipated (they had expected no more than a fight ending with the death of either Saucedo or Badillo) the woman had to set the next stage into motion. Crossing the clearing without so much as a backwards glance at the bodies, she went through the woodland to where a sergeant and corporal who served on Alvarez's staff were waiting with three horses.

'Is everything all right, *senora*?' the sergeant inquired.

'Perfect,' Beatriz answered. 'Help me mount and then go and do what the major told you!'

* Coup des deux veuves: *freely translated, the attack which causes two widows.*

191

After assisting the woman to board her horse's side-saddle, the soldiers swung astride their own mounts. On leaving the woodland, the trio split up. The sergeant galloped in the direction of the Tamaulipa Lancers' camp and the corporal went towards the lines of the 'Landero' Line Infantry Battalion. In accordance with their orders, they regulated their respective speeds so that they would arrive at their destinations practically simultaneously.

Following at a more leisurely pace, Beatriz watched the men and was satisfied that they were carrying out their instructions correctly. The *hacienda* hid the infantry encampment from her view, so she gave her attention to the sergeant. From her position, she could see several groups of Lancers scattered about their camp and guessed what the subject of their conversation must be. Her husband had had them informed, in Urrea's name, that the *cantina* would be closed and other restrictions enforced as punishment for the previous night's disturbance. The news was certain to increase their resentment and hatred of the foot soldiers, particularly as they had been left with the impression that Saucedo intended to use his rank to prevent the restrictions applying to his men.

Passing through the tent lines, the sergeant drew rein by a crowd consisting of officers and senior non-coms. Although the distance was too great for Beatriz to hear what was being said, she knew he was telling them that Saucedo had arrested Badillo at the *hacienda* and had taken him to the infantry lines. From all appearances, the news had the desired effect. Without asking questions, the party split up, the officers shouting orders. Rapidly arming themselves, the Lancers formed up on foot and headed toward their rivals' camp. Any doubts which might have lingered were washed away by the sight of the infantrymen, who had received the same news but in reverse, coming to meet them.

Satisfied that all was going as required, Beatriz passed

through the rear gate. Even as she rode towards the stables, shots sounded and were followed by shouts, screams of men in agony and the commotion of savage close-quarters fighting. The other arrangements were equally satisfactory. Her coach was outside the stables, its team hitched and under the supervision of two more members of her husband's staff.

'Is everything ready?' Beatriz demanded, dropping to the ground.

'Sí, senora,' the older man replied. 'All is loaded, but what's happening out—.'

'Don't let it bother you, it's nothing to do with us,' the woman answered, and looked around. 'Where is my husband?'

'He hasn't come back yet, senora,' the man answered, continuing to glance nervously in the direction of the disturbance.

'Are the gringos here?' Beatriz wanted to know.

'The big one and the Indian are in the stable, saddling their horses,' the man declared, showing agitation. 'But what about——.'

'Where is the other gringo?' Beatriz interrupted.

'He said he'd left something in his room and went back——,' the man began.

'Give me your pistol!' Beatriz snapped, holding out her right hand.

'Is something wr——?' the man gulped, but the urgency in the woman's tone made him respond to her demand.

'I don't know,' the woman admitted, turning and striding away. 'Stay here and be sure that everything is ready for us to move off as soon as we come back.'

❋　　❋　　❋　　❋　　❋

'Damn it, 'Cisco!' General José Urrea said irritably, stalking past his Paymaster towards the table in the centre of his sittingroom. He gestured towards the dispatch box that Alvarez had placed on it. 'I don't see why whatever it is can't wai——.'

Slipping the spear-pointed, razor sharp knife which he had used to murder Captain Seguin from its place of concealment up his left sleeve, the major thrust it deftly, almost hilt deep into the kidney region of his superior's back. The annoyed tirade ended as the pain of the completely unexpected attack tore through Urrea. Surprise, shock and anger warred with the agony that was distorting his face as his legs buckled and he crumpled dying to the floor. The searing torment that assailed him rendered him incapable of movement, and unable to cry out. Not that shouting would have helped. Before making his visit, Alvarez had ensured there was nobody else in that portion of the *hacienda*. Even the pretty serving woman with whom the General had been spending an afternoon of dalliance had been ordered by the Paymaster to return to the kitchen.

'No,' Alvarez answered, in a mocking tone, as he rolled the dying man over. 'And you never will.'

Having been called from his bed, the General had not troubled to don more than a shirt and a pair of trousers. There was a thin gold chain, from which a key was suspended, around his neck. When Alvarez reached towards it, Urrea made a feeble attempt to grab him. Showing no more hesitation or emotion than if he was butchering a pig, the Paymaster slit his all but helpless victim's throat. Ignoring the blood flooding from the hideous wound, he grasped and jerked the key free.

Turning away from the body, Alvarez crossed to a window and looked out. He saw the corporal riding into the infantry camp and let out a low curse. Waiting for Urrea to dismiss the serving woman had delayed the Paymaster longer than he had anticipated. He had wanted his business completed so that he was ready to leave as soon as the fighting broke out between the two regiments. However, he took some satisfaction from the

194

sight. Clearly there had been no hitch in Beatriz's part of the scheme. Now it was up to him to conclude his work so that they could be on their way as quickly as possible.

Striding to the table, he laid down the blood-smeared knife and picked up the dispatch box. He hurried to one of the room's three doors, entering what he knew was Urrea's bedroom. Going to the cupboard which ran along one side, he opened its door. Unlocking the massive strong box that was inside, he flung back the lid. Before removing any of the contents, he took a double-barrelled, percussion-fired pistol which had been part of the loot at Goliad from the dispatch case. Remembering what had happened during the interview with 'Smithers' that morning, he cocked back both hammers and placed the weapon close at hand on the floor.

Lifting a set of bulky saddlebags from the strong box, he set them down near the pistol. Then he started to transfer as much as he could of the jewellery and money from the strong box into the otherwise empty dispatch case. Once he stopped, thinking he heard a noise in the other room. His hand went to the butt of the pistol, but nothing happened to cause him further alarm. Deciding that the sound had been caused by Urrea, he went on with his looting. As he could not take all the contents of the strong box, he selected only the best. With the case filled, he closed its lid. Slinging the saddlebags over his shoulder, he tucked the case under his left arm and, with the pistol in his right hand, he took his departure.

A thought struck Alvarez as he returned to the sitting-room. When making his deal for an escort, an advance payment had been stipulated. While he felt sure that his wife could keep the *gringos* amicable, he did not consider it advisable to let 'Smithers' know just how much United States currency he had in his possession.

Setting his burdens on the table, Alvarez opened one

of the saddlebags and started to count out the required five hundred dollars. As he was doing so, he noticed that the main door was slightly ajar. The sight gave him a sensation similar to an ice cold hand touching his spine. Although he had not turned the key, he clearly remembered closing the door after sending the serving woman downstairs.

Even as the Paymaster started to consider the disturbing implications of his discovery, he heard the third door opening. Releasing the saddlebag, so that it fell and spilled a quantity of its contents on to the table, he snatched up his pistol. Lining it at the door, he let out a low and startled exclamation. 'Smithers' was stepping out of the suite's second bedroom.

'I thought you'd come up here,' Ole Devil remarked, wishing that he had taken the precaution of entering with the Manton held ready for use. Yet he realized that by coming out empty handed he might have saved himself from being shot on sight.

'You thought——?' the Paymaster began.

'Certainly,' Ole Devil went on, advancing a step and talking in the hope that he might distract Alvarez for long enough to take some more positive action. 'Even if he let you rob him, you couldn't chance leaving Urrea alive. He'd come after you with every man he could get. What's more, with him dead, Santa Anna would be satsified and wouldn't bother to try and capture somebody as harmless as you've always pretended to be. I came to see if you needed any help, but went into the wrong room.'

'That's an easy mistake to have made,' Alvarez admitted, noticing the way in which the *gringo* was looking at the money that had come from the open saddlebag.

Something in the Paymaster's tone brought Ole Devil's gaze from the table. What he read on the normally aesthetic face warned him that he was in great danger. Their eyes met and, as plainly as if the other had put the sentiment into words, Alvarez's expression said, 'So you've seen this money. Now I'll have to kill you.'

Knowing that he had no other choice, Ole Devil decided to gamble on diving aside in an attempt to avoid being shot. With the pistol's twin muzzles lined by a very steady hand at the centre of his chest, it was indeed a pitifully forlorn hope. At the first hint of movement he gave, Alvarez would complete the pressure on the trigger and liberate the hammer. Even if the first shot missed, there was a second barrel instantly available.

Watching the young Texian like a hawk, Alvarez made a correct guess at the thoughts which were passing through his head. With his right forefinger starting to tighten on the trigger, the Paymaster was alert and ready to counter whatever evasive action might be contemplated.

The room's main door began to open and the barrel of a pistol came into view!

Alvarez saw the movement and the weapon from the corner of his eye!

So did Ole Devil!

There was one difference. The Texian knew that, no matter who might be entering, it would not be one of his friends.

Although Ole Devil did not know how Alvarez intended to ensure their unimpeded departure, he had surmised that the hostility between the two regiments might be utilized in some way to create the necessary diversion. On commenting to the Paymaster about Beatriz's absence from the stable, he had been informed that she was still in their suite completing the last of the packing. Then, shortly after Alvarez had left, supposedly to collect her, her maid had arrived to ask if she had returned from the ride she had taken.

Still unaware of the exact plot, Ole Devil had guessed what had taken the Paymaster to the *hacienda*. So he had told his companions to remain with the horses while he went to investigate. He was confident that neither would go against his orders.

'Get him, Cousin Mylo!' Ole Devil yelled in his native tongue and dived to his left as he was speaking.

To give Alvarez credit, he responded with the speed of a striking diamondback rattlesnake. He also reacted as Ole Devil had hoped he would.

Speaking sufficient English to understand the Texian's meaning, the Paymaster concluded that the second *gringo* posed the greater and more immediate threat. Around snapped the twin barrelled pistol, lining towards the point where Alvarez estimated the person holding the other weapon would be. Flame and white smoke erupted from the right hand muzzle and the expelled bullet ripped a hole in the thin panelling of the door.

There was a cry of pain, proving that Alvarez had been correct—and lucky—in his aim. However, in the stress of the moment, he failed to notice that the cry had been feminine rather than masculine in timbre. Nor did he take any notice of the thud made by a body falling to the floor of the passage outside the room. He was too busy continuing with his plan to deal with 'Smithers'.

Going down, Ole Devil reached for and twisted free his pistol. He was moving with all possible speed, but knew it would be a very, *very*, close thing. Even as he hit the thick carpet and was turning the Manton forward, the Paymaster's weapon was swinging in his direction.

Jolted by his landing, although the thick covering over the boards of the floor reduced the force somewhat, Ole Devil kept a tight grip on the Manton's butt and, having used his left hand to cock the hammer, clamped it firmly on top of his right wrist for added security. There was no time to take a formal aim, so he looked along the barrel with both eyes open. Waiting until the weapon was partially concealing Alvarez's rage distorted face, forcing himself to ignore the ever increasing menace of the other's still potentially dangerous pistol, he squeezed the trigger.

Conscious of the Texian's weapon pointing at him, the Paymaster was also taking sight and making ready to shoot

Two lives were hanging in a very delicate balance!

The State of Texas—as it eventually became—had good cause to be grateful to Joseph 'Old Joe' Manton of London, England, that day. Such was his skilled craftsmanship that the superior mechanism of the pistol he had manufactured gave it a fractionally lighter trigger pull than the more cumbersome double-barrelled weapon. So the Manton spoke first.

Rising at an angle from the muzzle of Ole Devil's pistol, the bullet connected with the centre of Alvarez's forehead. It arrived just—and only just—in time. Lined accurately and with its trigger on the point of disengaging the hammer, the impact caused him to flinch and slightly turn his weapon.

Alvarez's lead came so close that it almost grazed Ole Devil's forehead and he felt the dust it kicked up from the carpet strike his cheek. Peering through the swirling powder's smoke, he saw the Paymaster pitching backwards.

Coming to his feet, with his left hand flashing to the bowie knife's hilt, Ole Devil looked to where Alvarez was sprawled supine. One glance told the Texian he had nothing further to fear from that source. Returning the pistol to its belt loop, he darted to the table. Listening for the first sounds which would warn him that the shooting had been heard and people were coming to investigate, he swept the coins back into the pouch. Still moving with haste, he closed and fastened the flap, then swung the saddlebags across his left shoulder. Picking up the dispatch box, he went to the door.

All was silent.

Ole Devil learned later that the whole of the domestic staff had been drawn from the house by the sound of fighting. As Urrea's suite was at the front of the building, the noise of the shooting had not carried to the rear.

On stepping cautiously into the passage, the Texian discovered the identity of his inadvertent saviour.

It was Beatriz Alvarez!

Coming to investigate the delay she had heard her husband and Ole Devil talking. She had tiptoed to the door with the intention of taking the latter by surprise. Instead of helping Alvarez, she had caused his and her own deaths. The Paymaster's bullet had lost little of its momentum while puncturing a way through the panelling of the door. Striking her under the right eye, it had still had sufficient impetus to range onwards and burst out of the top of her head.

Any remorse that Ole Devil might otherwise have experienced at having been the unwitting cause of the woman's death was lessened by the knowledge that she would not have hesitated to contribute to his own demise. Hurrying downstairs, he went through the deserted building and left by the rear door. At first he was alarmed by the sounds of fighting which came to his ears. Then, realizing that his own party could not be responsible for such a volume of noise, he guessed it was caused by the diversion Alvarez had arranged.

Looking worried, Mannen Blaze and Tommy Okasi were standing just inside the open doors of the stables holding the horses. Alvarez's sergeant and corporal had stayed clear of the fighting and had rejoined the other two enlisted men. Although they were staring at the back wall, they turned their attention to Ole Devil as he was approaching.

'Here, you four!' the Texian barked. 'Go up to the major's quarters and fetch the last of his baggage.'

For a moment, the quartet hesitated. Then the sergeant gave an order and they went towards the *hacienda*.

'Mount up,' Ole Devil told his companions. 'Our work's finished here.'

Five minutes later, while fighting was still raging between the remnants of the Tamaulipa Lancers and the 'Landero' Line Infantry Battalion, the three young men were riding north on the first stage of their journey back to Texas.

THE END

Author's note:—

*The reader may wonder, as I did, how Ole Devil
Hardin would have dealt with the situation if Major
Francisco Alvarez had been no more than he seemed.*

*Unfortunately, General Jackson Baines Hardin's as yet
unpublished autobiography—which I had the privilege
of reading while in Texas to attend Western Writers of
America's 21st Annual Convention—does not offer to
clear up that particular point. Although the General
was remarkably frank about most of his career, he wrote
little about the Urrea affair and none of it is speculative.
Nor do such official or private documents belonging to
Major General Samuel Houston and Presidente Antonio
Lopez de Santa Anna as are available give any greater
enlightenment. It is probable that any report made by
Ole Devil at the conclusion of the mission was verbal.
For obvious political—and possibly moral—reasons, none
of them wished to have details of such an assignment
committed to paper.*

*However, if Ole Devil's previous and subsequent career
is any criterion, one may feel sure that he would not
have hesitated to carry out his duty in any way possible. No matter what his personal feelings might have
been, faced with a potentially serious threat to the future
security and freedom of Texas, he would have taken any
necessary steps—not excluding assassination—to get
Urrea.*

J. T. Edson

BUNDUKI *by* J. T. Edson

A shot rang out . . . the driver slumped over the wheel . . .
suddenly the Land Rover began a three hundred foot dive
down the Gambuti Gorge to what should have been certain
death for both its passengers. But it wasn't . . .

Bunduki awoke in a strange country, dressed in a crudely
shaped leopard skin, and armed with primitive weapons.
Who had saved him? And why had they bothered to trans-
port him to this alien jungle, far away from Africa? And,
more important, had they also rescued his cousin, Dawn,
and was she, too, alone somewhere in this foreign land?
He had to find her and then maybe together they could
solve the mystery of their miraculous survival.

But first he had to overcome the dangers of the jungle—
a terrifying prospect for an ordinary man, but not for
Bunduki, adoptive son of Lord Greystoke—otherwise
known as *Tarzan of the Apes* . . .

0 552 09768 3—35p

WAR PARTY *by* Louis L'Amour

They were all rough, tough and ready to tangle . . .

BUD SHAW—the hired gun who found a victim worth saving . . .

LARK RILEY—the stranger with the hidden past—everybody wanted him to get out of town . . .

TELL SACKETT—he'd always fought shy of trouble, but now he was carrying other men's gold . . .

CHES LANE—Cochise's braves bushwhacked him then left him to a most unusual fate . . .

CAP MOFFIT—he made his name as cold-blooded killer, but there was one man he couldn't gun down . . .

WAR PARTY

0 552 09787 X—**40p**

SACKETT'S LAND *by* Louis L'Amour

BARNABAS SACKETT was a man of independent mind and independent spirit. His quick temper and deadly sword forced him to flee his English home and head out west.

Across the pirate-infested seas he traveled, to find fortune and adventure amid the unknown perils of the American frontier. For with the Indians, the gun-fighters, the rustlers and the bandits, it was a wild and dangerous land—a land that he intended to bend to his bold Sackett will—or die in the attempt . . .

This was

SACKETT'S LAND

0 552 098493—**40p**

YOUNG OLE DEVIL by J. T. Edson

'He's reckless, irresponsible and can't—or won't—avoid getting involved in fights no matter what duty he's supposed to be carrying out!'

That was the kind of comment which a senior officer of the Texas Light Cavalry might, with some justification, have made about hot-headed Lieutenant Red Blaze during the War between the States. However, it was uttered by Colonel William Barrett Travis shortly before his departure to take command of the garrison at the Alamo Mission in San Antonio de Bexar early in 1836. He was speaking about a young officer to whom Major General Samuel Houston intended to entrust a dangerous mission.

The officer in question was to become famous as the iron-hard disciplinarian who commanded the Confederate States Army of Arkansas and Northern Texas. His name was Jackson Baines Hardin—the man who became known as the 'lil ole devil' for fighting . . .

0 552 09650 4—**35p**

FIRST BLOOD by Jack Schaefer

Jess Harker was just edging past twenty and fed up to the teeth with driving the mail coach from Gap to Goshen and back. So when he was asked to take the main stage down to Stillwater with a record cargo of gold bullion he jumped at the chance. Billy Skinner and Race Crim decided to go along on the trip. Race was a veteran—no one stopped a stage when he was on the box.

But this time it was different . . . this time somebody had talked and the stage was ambushed at Big Creek. Billy Skinner was killed, and Jess lost a slice of rib. The robbers got the gold and Race—bent on revenge—took off into the hills with a hot gun, shooting wild at whatever came his way . . .

0 552 09821 3—**35p**

NEW ORLEANS GAMBLE *by* Louis Masterson

Owen Bellamy was a wanted man—an escaped convict, and the suspected murderer of Sheriff Alex Gorman. Gorman had boarded the riverboat 'Confederate Queen', hot on Bellamy's trail—and that was the last time he was seen alive. For when the 'Queen' docked the man matching Bellamy's description had vanished, and Gorman's body was washed ashore on the banks of the Mississippi.

The whole nasty business had become a federal affair—they needed an expert gambler, one who knew the Mississippi area like the back of his hand—someone who was prepared to face unknown danger and even death if Bellamy was to be brought to justice . . .

This was a job for one man alone—and that man was U.S. Marshal Morgan Kane . . .

0 552 09794 2—**30p**

APACHE *by* Louis Masterson

GERONOMO WAS ON THE WARPATH . . . killing . . . burning . . . looting, as once again the Apaches broke away from the reservation to wreak their own horrifying brand of destruction on the surrounding settlers. Somehow the U.S. Government had to get the situation under control —but first they had to smash the gun-running and illicit whiskey trade that put the weapons in the Indians' hands and the fire in their heads.

So Marshal Morgan Kane was ordered to head out to Arizona, and rustle up the bad men who were making profit out of murder. And that's when Morgan found himself in a whole lot of trouble . . . with the Indians, the army, and beautiful, fiery, Kate Coleman—the red-head who thought she could talk some sense into Geronomo . . .

0 552 09877 9—**35p**

A SELECTED LIST OF CORGI WESTERNS
FOR YOUR READING PLEASURE

GREAT LEGENDS OF THE WEST
☐ 09147 2	IN THE DAYS OF VICTORIO	*Eve Ball (illus.)*	40p
☐ 09095 0	APACHE	*Will Levington Comfort*	30p
☐ 09098 0	PAINTED PONIES	*Alan Le May*	35p
☐ 09097 2	VALLEY OF THE SHADOW	*Charles Marquis Warren*	35p

MORGAN KANE
☐ 08922 2	THE LAW OF THE JUNGLE No. 13	*Louis Masterson*	25p
☐ 08923 0	NO TEARS FOR MORGAN KANE No. 14	*Louis Masterson*	25p
☐ 09048 4	RIO GRANDE No. 17	*Louis Masterson*	25p
☐ 09328 9	THE BUTCHER FROM GUERRERO No. 22	*Louis Masterson*	25p
☐ 09256 5	HELL BELOW ZERO No. 25	*Louis Masterson*	30p
☐ 07274 5	SHANE	*Jack Schaefer*	30p
☐ 09311 4	THE KEAN LAND	*Jack Schaefer*	30p
☐ 09388 2	HIGH PLAINS DRIFTER	*Ernest Tidyman*	30p

J. T. EDSON
☐ 07840 9	THE REBEL SPY No. 1	*J. T. Edson*	35p
☐ 07844 1	THE TEXAN No. 3	*J. T. Edson*	35p
☐ 08012 8	SAGEBRUSH SLEUTH No. 24	*J. T. Edson*	35p
☐ 08064 0	THE TOWN TAMERS No. 31	*J. T. Edson*	35p
☐ 08065 9	GUN WIZARD No. 32	*J. T. Edson*	35p
☐ 09113 8	TWO MILES TO THE BORDER No. 70	*J. T. Edson*	25p

LOUIS L'AMOUR
☐ 09317 3	THE MAN CALLED NOON	*Louis L'Amour*	30p
☐ 09468 4	THE QUICK AND THE DEAD	*Louis L'Amour*	30p
☐ 09387 4	THE MAN FROM SKIBBEREEN	*Louis L'Amour*	30p
☐ 08995 8	CATLOW	*Louis L'Amour*	35p
☐ 08576 6	HANGING WOMAN CREEK	*Louis L'Amour*	35p
☐ 09264 9	THE FERGUSON RIFLE	*Louis L'Amour*	30p
☐ 09191 X	TREASURE MOUNTAIN	*Louis L'Amour*	30p

SUDDEN
☐ 08812 9	SUDDEN MAKES WAR	*Oliver Strange*	30p
☐ 08810 2	SUDDEN—OUTLAWED	*Oliver Strange*	30p
☐ 08907 9	SUDDEN—TROUBLESHOOTER	*Frederick H. Christian*	30p
☐ 09170 7	SUDDEN—DEAD OR ALIVE	*Frederick H. Christian*	30p

All these books are available at your bookshop or newsagent: or can be ordered directly from the publisher. Just tick the titles you want and fill in the form below.

CORGI BOOKS, Cash Sales Department, P.O. Box 11, Falmouth, Cornwall.
Please send cheque or postal order, no currency. **U.K. and Eire** send 15p for first book plus 5p per copy for each additional book ordered to a maximum charge of 50p to cover the cost of postage and packing. **Overseas Customers and B.F.P.O.** allow 20p for first book and 10p per copy for each additional book.

NAME (Block letters) ....

ADDRESS ....

(AUG. 75) ....

While every effort is made to keep prices low, it is sometimes necessary to increase prices at short notice. Corgi Books reserve the right to show new retail prices on covers which may differ from those previously advertised in the text or elsewhere.